A Wicked Good Play

by Tony Burton

God bless!
Tony Burton

Wolfmont

This is a work of fiction. Names, characters, places and incidents are either the product of the author's imagination or are used fictitiously, and any resemblance to actual persons, living or dead, business establishments, events or locales is entirely coincidental.

A WICKED GOOD PLAY

First printing – December 2005
Wolfmont Publishing,
Copyright ©2005 Tony Burton
All Rights Reserved

ISBN 1-4116-7166-X

This book may not be reproduced in whole or in part, by mimeograph, photocopy, or any other means, electronic or physical, without express written permission of the author.

For information, contact:
info@wolfmont.com
or
Wolfmont Publishing
PO Box 205
Ranger, GA   30734

Dedicated to my own two lovely daughters,
Shanna and Patricia,
who have brought their father much joy

Chapter 1

Thou shalt not be afraid for the terror by night; nor for the arrow that flieth by day; Nor for the pestilence that walketh in darkness; nor for the destruction that wasteth at noonday.
Psalms 91:5,6

The crashing sound of a gunshot jarred the darkness, and Rev. Thomas Wilson was jerked awake. He quickly switched on the lamp beside his bed and sat upright, his mind in a tailspin. What was going on? Were they in danger? Then there was another reverberating gunshot, and the throaty roar of an accelerating engine, followed closely by the sound of squealing tires.

As the cobwebs of sleep cleared from his mind, he remembered - he was in bed, Amy was asleep beside him, and their adopted baby daughter Deanna was snuggled into her crib just inches from his side. As he looked at the two of them, blissfully unaware of any disturbances, he marveled again at how alike they were even though they had no blood connection whatsoever. Both slept like the proverbial rock, and it took more than a loud noise to wake either of them.

Thomas sighed, and threw the covers back from his legs, stepping out onto the carpet. Now that he had his wits about him, he figured he knew the cause for the gunshots and tire-squealing departure.

It was early November, and deer hunting season was in full swing. Thomas didn't mind that - he had eaten his share of venison jerky, barbecued venison, deerburgers, and so forth. But this year several large deer had been seen in the field across the road from the church and parsonage, and this was the second time this month he had been blasted awake by someone trying to "spotlight" a deer late at night.

"The Lord is my shepherd, I shall not want," Thomas muttered with irritation as he shuffled through the house. That Psalm always helped to calm him. Thomas was not easily angered, but he found it inexcusable that so-called sportsmen would attempt to shine a bright light into a deer's eyes to confuse and temporarily paralyze it, then shoot it while it was in this state of semi-stupefaction. That wasn't sporting - it wasn't even legal, for goodness sake.

That was why he was calling 9-1-1 right now, as he poured himself a glass of milk.

The bored-sounding emergency operator answered, "Cuthbert County Emergency Services. May I help you?"

"Yes, I'd like to report shots fired from the road in front of my house. They sounded like a high-powered rifle. They were followed by the sound of someone taking off in a car or truck, squealing their tires."

"Is anyone there injured, sir?" There was a little more concern in the voice now.

"No one in my house is injured. I was awakened and startled, that's all."

"Did any bullets strike the house, sir?"

"I have no idea. I didn't notice any, but it's 2:40 AM, and I'm not going out there in my pajamas to check."

"Alright sir, we'll have someone drive by and check it out. Is there anything else?"

"No, thanks. That was it."

"Thank you, sir." The emergency operator said, then hung up.

Thomas padded into the living room that faced the road, and peered out the window into the moonlit night, sipping his cold milk. He couldn't see any dark shapes lying in the pasture, so he hoped the poaching hunters missed whatever they were aiming at.

As he stood in the darkened living room, he marveled at the beauty of the night, even when it had just been disturbed by the intrusion of man's callous disregard for fair play and for the law. But suddenly his attention was drawn to a part of the pasture near an adjoining woods. There was a figure moving there, but it didn't look like a deer. It looked like a human being.

Thomas peered more closely through the breath-fogged window. Yes, that was definitely a person, although he could not have said whether male or female, young or old. The person stood at the edge of the woods for a few moments, then jumped up and down, flinging its arms about in a strange exuberance. Thomas's jaw dropped.

The figure stopped it's strange dance and faded back into the darkness of the woods. Though Thomas stood there straining his eyes for several minutes, he saw no more of the odd figure.

He blinked several times to clear his vision and peered again at the field, but was interrupted in his visual search by the arrival of a county police cruiser. The black-and-white Ford LTD pulled into the driveway of the parsonage, and two officers got out. He hurried to the door so they wouldn't ring the doorbell and possibly awaken Amy. She was conditioned to that, for some reason - it would awaken her, as would the phone, even though thunder, gunshot or other loud noises usually would not.

The two officers came in, taking off their hats, and introduced themselves as Officers Huffington and Riesling.

"We understand you reported some gunfire in front of your house. Can you tell us about it?" Officer Huffington said, as his partner took out a notepad.

"About 25 minutes ago, I was awakened by a very loud gunshot. It sounded to my ears like a high-powered rifle - something like a .30-30 or a .30-06. I sat up in bed, and there was another gunshot, within ten to fifteen seconds of the first one.

"Right after the second gunshot, I heard the sound of an accelerating engine with a loud muffler and the squeal of tires. I got up and looked out the window, but couldn't see any car or truck," Thomas stated.

Both officers nodded, and Riesling asked, "Did you see anyone or anything unusual after the car left?"

"Well, you know, it is odd, but I wasn't sure if I wanted to mention this. There are several large whitetail deer that have shown up in the field across the road," and he gestured in that direction. "Someone was out there about a week ago trying to spotlight a deer. That time I saw the vehicle, but not clearly enough to get a good description or a license plate number. I figured that was what happened tonight, too.

"But as I was waiting for you two to arrive, I was standing by the front door and looking out the window at the pasture where the deer normally show up. As you can see, it's a brightly moonlit night. I didn't see any deer, but after a few minutes I saw what looked like a person come out of the woods beside the pasture." He stopped, uncertain how to finish.

The officers both reacted to this news with increased alertness, like two hounds who caught a scent. Huffington asked, "What did the person do, Reverend?"

"That's the really odd part," Thomas said, "and I can't explain it. This person, whoever he or she was, came out of the woods, paused a few seconds, and then jumped up and down, flapping their arms. Whether they were trying to get warm, or celebrate, or dance, I have no idea!" He looked at both men, whose level gazes gave away nothing about what might be going through their minds. "After a few moments of that, the person stopped and went back into the woods. A little later, you two drove up in your police car."

Officer Riesling cleared his throat. "Ah, I see. Well, I'll go out and check by the road to see if I can find any signs, while my partner checks the front of your house to see if he can see any bullet damage." With that, both men replaced their caps and went outside. Thomas stood on their front steps in his pajamas and a terrycloth robe, watching Riesling checking the road with a flashlight, while Huffington investigated the front of the house.

In about five minutes Officer Riesling returned to the door and entered. "There are fresh tire marks on the road that indicate someone left here in a hurry not long ago, although I didn't see any spent rounds." He shrugged. "They may have been ejected into the interior of the vehicle." He started to turn away, then stopped and asked, "Did anyone else hear or see the gunshots or the vehicle?"

"I don't think so, Officer - at least not here in this house. My wife and baby both sleep like logs, and when I woke up they didn't stir at all." The officer raised his eyebrows at this, but Thomas nodded his head. "Oh, yes, Officer. My wife will waken at the phone, the doorbell, or the cry of the baby, but just about nothing else will disturb her when she is solidly asleep. She's been that way for years."

Officer Huffington returned then, his shoes wet with dew and covered with little pieces of cut grass from the lawn. "There are no signs of any bullet damage to the house, Reverend, at least not as far as I can see."

"I didn't expect there would be," Thomas replied. "Like I said, I believe they were trying to shoot a deer illegally."

"Well, whatever they were trying to do, it was illegal," replied Riesling. "Hunting deer more than thirty minutes after sundown is illegal. Hunting within 100 yards of a public thoroughfare is illegal. Firing a weapon from a vehicle is illegal. And disturbing the peace is illegal. So, they are in trouble one way or another, IF we can catch them."

"And how likely do you think that is, realistically?" Thomas asked.

Officer Riesling grinned humorlessly at him. "Well, that's the point, isn't it? We really don't have a lot to go on, but every time a report like this comes in we get a little more information, and maybe it will all add up eventually. So, I'd say keep your eyes open for anyone who may stop and seem to be examining that field too closely." He paused. "You know what I mean - seeing what they might be able to shoot, if they had the chance."

"What about the person who came out of the woods and did a little dance? Is that going to be investigated?" Thomas asked.

The two officers looked at each other, then Huffington said, "Well, as far as we can determine, that person, whoever he or she may be, didn't break any law or cause any trouble. We really have no reason to investigate who they may be, or what they might have been doing, sir."

Thomas opened his mouth to speak, then closed it as he realized they were perfectly right. Strange, even downright nutty behavior, wasn't necessarily a reason for a police investigation as long as no one was endangered or injured. So he just said, "Well, thank you, officers. Do I need to sign anything now?"

Huffington shook his head. "No, sir. We have to type up the report, and you can come in and sign it sometime in the next two or three days. We won't have it complete before the day after tomorrow, anyway."

"Ah, OK, then." He yawned. "I think I'll try to get back to sleep. I hope the rest of your shift is quiet, gentlemen. God bless you and keep you both safe!" The men touched their caps in a sort of salute, and left, with Thomas shutting and locking the door behind them.

Thomas returned to bed as he heard the police car pulling away from their driveway. He lay there in the darkness, listening to the sound of Amy breathing, and the lighter, faster echo of that sound from little Deanna. Thank God they hadn't been endangered!

He stood up again, going over to the side of Deanna's crib. He reached down and rested his hand lightly on her chest, feeling the swift rise and fall of her ribs, and the light "tap-tap" of her tiny heartbeat. He smiled in the darkness, thinking of the wonder of the little life there, and the joy that God had given them by allowing them to adopt this beautiful child.

Father, he prayed, *make me always mindful of the blessings you have given us, and most especially of the blessing of those we love and who love us. Don't let me fall into the habit of taking that love for granted, Lord.*

He bent over and kissed Deanna's forehead. She puckered up in a little frown, but relaxed again with a sigh. Thomas returned to bed then, comforted both by his faith and by the warm feeling of being surrounded by those he loved, his baby daughter on one side and his wife on the other. With that happy thought in his mind, he drifted off to sleep.

* * *

The next morning dawned cool and clear, and Thomas had a little trouble getting out of bed with his loss of sleep. But Deanna helped with that. As soon as she heard the alarm clock begin its raucous buzz, she opened her eyes and added her voice to the din. Breakfast was always high on her list of priorities when she awakened, it seemed, and today was no exception.

But Amy was a step ahead of her. Just as Thomas rolled out of bed and leaned across into the crib to comfort Deanna, Amy walked in with a bottle in one hand and a cup of coffee in the other. "Here you go, Thomas. I've already had mine," she said as she handed him the steaming mug. She picked up Deanna and offered her the breakfast bottle, which the hungry baby immediately accepted.

After a couple of minutes of ravenous sucking sounds coming from Deanna and her bottle, accompanied by murmured endearments from Amy, she turned to Thomas and asked, "Did something happen last night that I don't know about? I seem to vaguely remember you getting up out of bed, and there is a lot less milk in the 'fridge than there was last night after supper!"

Thomas laughed. "Well, yes, something did happen. I'm surprised you remember anything about it, though. I thought you were dead to the world." He told her about the gunshot that woke him, and about the subsequent visit by the police. He also told her about the strange figure he saw dancing or jumping at the edge of the woods, and her eyebrows rose.

"There was someone there at 2:45 in the morning?" she asked in amazement. "Are you sure?"

He nodded his head. "Yes, I am sure. You're giving me the same sort of look the police officer gave me, honey! I was awake, not sleepwalking." He grinned, then got up and went into the bathroom to get started with the day.

Later, showered and dressed, Thomas decided to see what he could find across the road. He donned some sneakers and a jacket, and carefully navigated his way through the barbed-wire fence around the pasture. The pasture owner had already sold off this year's beef cattle, so the pasture was empty. He headed in the general direction of where he saw the jumping figure, and saw several indications along the way that deer had been recently feeding there.

He walked along the edge of the forest, looking for any signs of the phantom dancer, but at first was frustrated. He walked about one hundred yards, and decided to call it quits. But on his way back, he noticed the pine needles were disturbed in an area at one point, and as he approached, he saw the distinct imprint of a sneaker in the clay soil beneath. It was the toe of the sneaker only, which he thought would be reasonable if the wearer were jumping up and down.

Satisfied now that he definitely had seen the strange, exultant figure (he was beginning to wonder!), he made his way back to the parsonage and informed Amy of what he found. She acted surprised that he went to the trouble to verify what he saw, but was just as puzzled as he by the idea of someone jumping up and down in the edge of a pasture at 2:45 AM on a Tuesday morning.

"Thomas, Father McClenny called to remind you of the Interfaith Initiative meeting this afternoon," she said as she handed him the paper where she wrote down the particulars of the phone call.

"Oh, right! It's being held at Temple Beth Shalom this month. I hadn't totally forgotten, but I have to admit it wasn't at the top of my memory."

"Isn't that where Larry Meyer attends services?" Amy asked.

"Yes, it is. They have a very nice facility there, with a K-12 school as well as the normal synagogue facilities," Thomas replied

"Don't go getting ideas about putting a K-12 school into our new church building! We have enough worries with just building the new sanctuary, Christian education center and fellowship hall!" Amy looked at him with mock horror.

"Actually, I was thinking about starting our own Bible college and seminary!" he teased her.

That afternoon, he went to the monthly meeting of the Interfaith Initiative at 1:30, and it was over by 3:00. He was surprised to meet Larry Meyer in the hallway as he was leaving.

"Larry, how are you? Not working today?" Thomas asked.

"The second pharmacist is taking care of things for an hour or two while I look in on my daughter Esther. She's in a play here at the school, and they are practicing this afternoon. I wanted to sneak around and watch her while she is practicing, you know? I didn't want her to know I was here because it might make her nervous," Larry explained.

"Really? What play are they performing?"

"It's an Agatha Christie play, 'Ten Little Indians'. She is playing this really up-tight religious woman who is a big hypocrite." He grinned at Thomas. "Luckily, she's not identified as any particular faith, other than she quotes the Bible a lot."

"I remember seeing a movie by that name. It was an old black-and-white movie, though, from the Forties," Thomas said.

"Well, they're just getting started practicing, I think. Want to go and spy on them with me?"

Thomas agreed and walked along with Larry to a door that led to stairs which went up to a small balcony area looking down on a stage. They quietly took their seats and watched.

The first scene was sort of slow at first. It was primarily setting the tone of the play, and introducing all the main characters, which were ten in all.

Larry nudged Thomas when his daughter came out onto the stage. "There she is," he whispered.

The last time Thomas had seen Esther was about six months ago, but she grew a lot during that time and he didn't think he would have recognized her. It gave him a warm feeling to think that he might be experiencing the same sort of fatherly pride in his own daughter in a few years.

The young actors had practiced a lot, it was obvious, but it was interesting to see how the director was stopping things and advising them on how to get the most out of their parts. All the kids were nervous, but none were reading their parts, although a few did have to be prompted at one point or another.

Finally, it came time for the climax of the first act. A handsome young man, playing the callow and detestable Anthony Marston, flawlessly executed his lines and tossed back a pretend glass of whiskey.

He grasped his throat, then his stomach, and arched his back, then fell to the floor rolling and retching.

"Cut! Stop, stop!" the director, a young woman of about thirty yelled. "Eddie, for goodness sake, what was THAT?" she demanded.

The young actor raised himself up onto his elbow and said, "What was what?"

"What was all that contorting and thrashing around?" his director asked, obviously displeased. "You're supposed to be dying from cyanide, not having a fit!"

The rest of the young cast giggled, and the erstwhile corpse grinned. "Well, I was trying for something more dramatic this time!"

"OK, well, how about trying a different way to be dramatic? Why don't you go to Mrs. Kniebel, the science teacher, and ask her how a cyanide poisoning would affect someone? Dramatic is good, but let's think about realistic, too. Then, come back and we'll talk about it, OK?"

The young man got up, brushed off his clothes and went off, supposedly to find the science teacher.

The practice continued, but in a short while Thomas looked at his watch and realized he was going to be late for dinner if he didn't leave now. He still needed to run a couple of errands before heading home. Whispering a goodbye to Larry, he stood up to leave, but Larry followed him out.

"So, what do you think?" Larry asked, fully the proud papa.

"I think, with a little more practice, they're going to be great!"

"Listen, the performance is going to be on Thursday night, Saturday night, and on Sunday night, next week. I'll get a couple of tickets for you and Amy, if you'd like to come see it," Larry offered.

Thomas smiled, both at the offer and at Larry's obvious pride in his daughter's acting. "Sure, Larry! We'd be honored to see the play."

"Great, then. What night is best?"

Thomas thought for a second, and said, "Thursday, I think. Saturday's are always busy with preparation for the next day's service."

Larry nodded, said "Thursday night, then," and returned to his perch in the balcony. Thomas ran his errands, and hurried, but it was still growing dusk as he approached his home. He pulled into the driveway, stopped the car and got out, then stood absolutely still. Those deer were in the field across the road again, and he was always entranced by their graceful movements and beauty. Thomas finally shook off the charm of the creatures and went inside with the bags of groceries.

Chapter 2

Therefore sent he thither horses, and chariots, and a great host: and they came by night, and compassed the city about.
                                                                                II Kings 6:14

Thomas walked into the house with the bags of groceries from Wiggleston's. The warm, moist air of the kitchen, redolent with the smell of homemade soup, made him immediately relaxed and ravenous.

Amy was in the dining room, with Deanna in a baby carrier in front of her, playing baby games with her. "Hi, honey," she said, as she covered her eyes for another round of "Where's the baby?"

Thomas swung the refrigerator open and placed the milk and eggs inside it. He went over to the table and delivered a kiss to both his wife and daughter, then sat down beside them.

"I just saw more deer in the pasture across the road. They are beautiful creatures! But there wasn't anyone else there, this time, only the deer."

Amy looked sideways at him. "Honey are you sure there was anyone there last time?"

"Oh, ha-ha! Very funny... but I did see that person last night at the edge of the forest. Remember, I told you how I found the footprints up there this morning!"

Amy giggled. "Thomas, you know I was only teasing you. Of course I believe you. But I still wonder why a person would be up there like that, jumping up and down and waving their arms. Do you have any ideas?" She stood up, went over to check the soup on the stove, and turned the heat down a little, then stood leaning against the cabinets, looking curiously at Thomas.

Thomas was now involved in playing baby games, so he didn't notice her inquiring look. She cleared her throat, and he looked at her.

"Oh, I don't know. I can't figure it out, either. I only know what I saw." He shrugged. "I guess it isn't very important, but it really puzzled me last night." He picked Deanna up and stood gently rocking her to and fro as he continued.

"Oh, by the way, I saw Larry Meyer today."

"Really? Was he at the Interfaith Initiative meeting, too?"

"No, his daughter goes to school there. Remember meeting Esther? Well, she is also in a school play they are presenting there this month, and Larry asked me to go into the balcony and watch his daughter with him." Thomas dropped his voice to a secretive stage whisper. "We were spying on her!" He laughed, then resumed his normal voice. "He didn't want to make her nervous, so we watched from the darkness of the balcony."

"What play is it?" Amy asked as she ladled soup from the stockpot into two bowls, and placed cheese sandwiches onto plates.

Thomas placed Deanna back into her baby carrier, and went about the preparation of something to drink for them both. "It's an Agatha Christie play, called 'Ten Little Indians'. I remember seeing a black-and-white version of it as a movie, a few years ago." He placed the filled glasses on the table beside the plates. "Larry invited us to the play, and said he would get tickets for us if we wanted. It's next Thursday night. I said yes. Any objections?"

Amy shook her head as she sat down. "No, sounds great!" She laughed. "You know, I just realized something. Now, we have to think about something totally new when we are going out: we have to find a babysitter!"

Thomas sat in silence for a few seconds as that sank in. Deanna had only been theirs for a few months now, and he still sometimes had a hard time thinking of himself as a father. He bowed his head and gave thanks for their meal, adding a special thanks for being able to worry about such a thing as "having a babysitter."

They started eating, and in a few moments Amy said, "You know, I think I saw that play a long time ago. But it wasn't called 'Ten Little Indians'. I mean, there were ten little Indian statuettes in it, but it was called 'And Then There Were None.' It was an enjoyable play, sort of a dark comedy in ways."

"Well, I think it will be good for us to go and see it," Thomas said. "How long has it been since we were at a live performance of a play, anyway?"

She looked up at him with a ghost of a grin. "You mean, other than a Christmas play with little shepherds wearing old draperies, and with towels wrapped around their heads?" She chuckled. "It's been a long time."

Later, about eleven o'clock, Thomas carried the garbage out to put it in the big dumpster behind the church. When he came back to the parsonage, he glanced up at the field, more by habit than anything else. Thomas froze in his tracks.

Across the road there were three or four whitetail deer in the pasture, just as he had seen at other times lately. One possessed a very large set of antlers. The deer alone didn't surprise him. What surprised him was what appeared to be a person standing in the middle of them, with a hand resting on the back of the large buck!

The evening mist rose within minutes from the damp pasture, and hid both the deer and the mysterious figure. Try as he might, he couldn't make out their shapes any more, so he went inside.

"I just saw the strangest thing," he said as he shut the door. "There were four large deer in the pasture across the road. But they weren't alone: standing in the middle of them was what appeared to be a human being, and it looked like he, or she, had their hand resting on the back of one of the deer!"

Amy just turned and looked at him, then shook her head in mock pity. "Honey, it's just the lack of sleep. Get enough rest tonight, and you won't be seeing funny dancing guys out playing with the deer." She ran out of the room laughing, with Thomas chasing her in mock fury, but they both stopped just short of waking Deanna.

The next morning, Thomas went to the Cuthbert County Police Department to see and sign his incident report from two nights before. Neither officer was there, being assigned to the night shift this week, but a friend of his, Detective Lt. Eric Lamonde, was working.

"Thomas! Good to see you again." Eric took Thomas's hand and shook it. "What brings you here?"

"I need to sign an incident report, Eric. Officers Huffington and Riesling took the report a couple of nights ago."

17

Eric frowned. "Something happening there at the new church site?" He led the way to his office as he spoke, and asked an administrative assistant there to bring him the incident report.

Thomas shook his head. "No, Eric, nothing like that. But somebody has been trying to spotlight the deer in the field across from the parsonage, late at night. I've been awakened twice now by people trying to spotlight deer there." Thomas sat down in the chair Eric offered him. "It's not sporting, and besides, shooting a high-powered rifle from a vehicle on the highway is both illegal and very dangerous!"

Eric was nodding as Thomas said this. The administrative assistant brought the report in and gave it to him, and Eric scanned it quickly. He stopped in mid-page and slowly looked up at Thomas. He returned his gaze to the report sheet, and read it again. He cleared his throat.

"Ahhh... Thomas, what's this about someone dancing around in the field?" Eric's voice held a note of skepticism, mixed with humor.

The minister took a deep breath. People just didn't seem to want to believe him! "Eric, I am not making it up. I saw that person, whoever it was, leaping up and down and waving their arms at the edge of the woods." Thomas's voice grew more defensive.

"And yesterday morning, I went over to double-check, just to make sure my eyes weren't deceiving me. Sure enough, I found the impression of a sneaker in the clay near the edge of the woods, formed just the way a person would if they were jumping up and down."

Eric was grinning at Thomas, and suddenly Thomas realized that he had been teased. He chuckled, and Eric joined him.

"Thomas, after our first encounter together, I've learned to try very hard to believe what you say, even when it sounds far-fetched. I just wanted to rag you a little!" Eric was enjoying himself.

Thomas laughed, too, but put up a hand. "Wait, there's more! Last night, I came home just as it was getting on to twilight. There were a couple of deer in the pasture across the road, which isn't unusual. One of them was a big buck."

Eric was nodding, his eyes narrowed as he waited for the punchline.

Thomas continued, "But here's the strange part: later last night, when I took out the garbage, there was a larger herd, maybe three or four. And in the middle of this small herd of deer was a person, standing. The person appeared to have his, or her, hand resting on the back of the big buck!" Thomas finished and leaned back in his chair, arms crossed as though daring Eric to disagree with him.

Eric was totally silent for a few seconds, the only noises the sounds of muffled conversations and ringing phones from the rest of the police department. Then he cleared his throat.

"Uh-huh. Well. That IS very unusual." Eric was obviously at a loss for words.

Thomas leaned forward. "Eric, I want you to believe me, because it is the truth. But, as far as I can see, it's not that important anyway. No crime is being committed by this person, whoever they are. The land is not posted, only marked 'No Hunting.' This person apparently is not hunting the deer. I only brought it up with the officers the other night because I thought it was strange, and because, with a person is up there like that, anyone trying to shoot at a deer could kill them, even if by accident.

"So, as long as the police department can stop the poachers from trying to spotlight deer at night, that should also remove the danger to whoever it is up there with the whitetail deer." Thomas sat back in his chair.

Eric regarded him for a few seconds, then nodded. "Well, you're right, of course. Still, this really seems strange to me – and it has me very curious." He passed the report over to Thomas, who read through it and signed it.

As he passed the report back to Eric, he asked, "So, what will the police do about the poachers?"

The detective looked at Thomas a little shamefacedly. "The truth? Probably very little. It's a low priority with the department right now. We've had a series of break-ins, and the mayor and county commissioner are riding our backs to solve them."

Thomas nodded. "I've read about them in the newspaper, and one of our members has been a victim, too. But if the police department isn't going to do anything, what do you recommend?"

"Hey, wait a sec.! I didn't say we weren't going to do anything! I said 'very little'." He studied Thomas for a minute. "Thomas, do you have bright lights, maybe floodlights, in the front part of your house or property, close to the road?"

Thomas nodded. "Yes, we have some security lights. Why?"

"Well, people who spotlight deer know they are breaking the law, so they don't want to be identified. Bright lights will make them nervous about stopping and shooting. And, they may make the deer nervous about being so close to the road, too." He shrugged.

"Until they free patrolmen up from this break-in scare, that's my best recommendation. That, and of course, trying to get a good look at anyone who still tried to shoot a deer at night. A description of the vehicle would be good, a license plate number would be excellent. Even a patrolman coming by there would be unlikely to pass at the exact time the poachers were there. You are there more than anyone else right now." He sipped his coffee, then made a face. "Ack, it's cold!" He looked at Thomas. "Want some coffee? I need to freshen this."

"No, thanks, Eric. I need to get back home. We have mid-week service tonight, and I still have a couple things I want to prepare." He stood up and turned to the door. "You know you and your wife are still welcome to visit our church any time."

Eric nodded, smiling. "I know, Thomas. Thanks for reminding me, though."

On the way home, Thomas mulled over the strange person in the pasture. While stopped at a red light, a battered red pickup truck pulled up beside him. The day was unusually warm for early November, so Thomas was driving with his window down. But the truck that sat beside him now had a very loud engine, as well as a bass-booming stereo system. They probably need it that loud to hear it over the engine, Thomas thought as he quickly rolled up his window. The sound wasn't kept out, but at least diminished.

When the light turned green, the driver of the red truck punched the accelerator and his truck roared like it was angry, and after a second of delay, the back tires spun and squealed. The truck took off, and Thomas looked up in surprise. That sounded exactly like the one that took off from in front of his house the other night!

He accelerated a little to catch up, but mud obscured most of the license plate. He memorized the numbers he saw there, so he could write them down later. He looked up, and with a sort of warped satisfaction he saw a scoped rifle hanging across the back window of the pickup. Maybe he was right.

But he couldn't afford the time to try to follow the loud, dirty truck right now. A little frustrated, he turned aside onto Highway 62, toward home.

After that night's service, several of the church members went out to a fast-food restaurant to relax and fellowship a little. As they sat eating french fries, the conversation between the men turned to deer hunting season.

"Well, I didn't see a single deer last year, much less shoot anything," grumbled Bob Gramm. "I don't know if I'm even going to go hunting this year. It's cold and uncomfortable in a deer stand at 5:30 in the morning, and I'd much rather mooch some venison from one of you three mighty hunters!" He gestured around at Simon Daniels, Stan Bowman and Jack Stansell. The three of them grinned; they all had reputations as hunters who never failed to bring home at least one deer each season, if not two or more.

Thomas washed down his last bite. "You know how I told you that those deer have been showing up in the field across from the church and parsonage?" The men at the table all nodded. "Well, someone has tried twice in the last couple of weeks to spotlight one, in the middle of the night. The gunshots woke me up out of a sound sleep."

The men were all surprised at first, but Stan nodded. "I've heard of people doing that around here before. Of course, you never know *who* does it: it's always, 'I know someone whose cousin does that...', you know?" He wadded up his food wrappers. "Makes me mad, too. It's not sporting, it's illegal and it's doggone dangerous, too. Most of the time the people who do that are shooting from a vehicle on a public road!"

Thomas told them of his trip to the police department that day, and of the advice to turn on the bright security lights at the front of the parsonage, to try to discourage the poachers. This received general approval, and when he and Amy left, he was determined to keep the lights on throughout the hunting season, if necessary.

That night, after Amy tucked Deanna into bed, Thomas went to the utility room and turned on the bright halogen security lights that illuminated the front of the parsonage and the driveway. He checked out the window for the amount of illumination, and was pleased at the result.

No screeching tires, roaring engines or gunshots interrupted their sleep that night or the next. But at about 3:00 AM Saturday morning, Thomas was startled awake by a series of gunshots, the sound of something hitting the side of their house, and the sudden absence of light through the front blinds.

A roaring engine, screeching tires and a raucous electronic car horn playing the "Charge!" bugle call completed his wake-up call. Rushing to the front door, he stepped outside in his pajamas and robe. It was dark out front now, so he retrieved a flashlight and found that the front of their home had been peppered with buckshot, taking out the two center security lights and pockmarking the brick wall.

Chapter 3

For now we see through a glass, darkly; but then face to face: now I know in part; but then shall I know even as also I am known.

I Corinthians 13:12

Thomas had Amy move herself and Deanna to a room in the back part of the house, while he called the police. They were much quicker to respond this time, with two patrol cars instead of one.

Officer Riesling was in one car, and another officer whom Thomas had not met before was in the other. Soon another car arrived with a couple of detectives, one of whom began taking photographs of the wall, the broken lights, and all around the house.

Detective Davis introduced himself and came into the parsonage, sitting on the sofa. Amy came out briefly, just to state that she had been asleep for the gunshots both this time and the past time, although Thomas awakened her when he bounded from the bed. Davis took her statement, and she went back to console a now-fussy Deanna.

"So, you're saying this is the third time in the last month you have been awakened by gunshots at night like this?" he asked.

Thomas nodded. "Yes, but I only reported the last one and this one. I went by and signed the report just a couple of days ago. Detective Lamonde was there when I signed the report, and he gave me a copy of it. Would you like to see it?"

The detective shook his head. "No, I'll get a copy when I get back to the station. Is this the first time that the perpetrators have fired at your home?"

"Yes, thank God, it's the first time and I hope it is the last! I think they were deliberately aiming to shoot out the security lights." Thomas paused. "Detective Lamonde advised me to turn on bright lights that shone out onto the road and the field, if I had any, saying that it might discourage the poachers as well as tend to keep the deer further away from the road." He looked down at his hands. "It's obvious these people aren't intimidated by bright lights!"

Detective Davis nodded as he kept taking notes. "Do you have any idea who may have been doing this? Have you received any threats, or made any new enemies?"

Thomas just looked at Davis for a moment, then replied, "I don't think this is so much an attack on me as it is a way to stop me from 'interfering' with their nighttime poaching. As for suspicions, I did notice a vehicle yesterday that sounded a lot like the vehicle that has been here two times before." He described the beat-up looking red pickup he had seen, described how it hesitated before taking off just like the ones he heard before, and gave what he saw of the license number.

Davis nodded as he took all this down, then looked up at Thomas. "You realize, this is pretty thin. But we can try to check up on the vehicle, see what matches up, that sort of thing. Don't bet too heavily on it!"

Thomas was about to tell Detective Davis about the strange figure near the deer, but stopped before bringing the subject up. He hadn't seen the person tonight, so it was not a part of the incident. And he really didn't relish getting that look from the officer that silently said, "Another looney!"

Detective Davis stood up to leave. "I recommend you sleep in a back bedroom of the house tonight, if possible. They probably wouldn't return tonight, but it's better to be safe. The report will be available for you, for purposes of insurance claims and that sort of thing, by Tuesday afternoon. Just come by the police station and they'll copy it for you.

"Also, we'll double up on patrols by here for a few days. You should see a black-and-white going by here at least five or six times a day while that's happening." He closed his notebook. "We'll do everything we can to catch these people, Reverend Wilson. Believe me, poaching deer with a spotlight is one thing, but when people start firing shotguns at homes, that gets our full attention."

Thomas walked the detective to the door, where he joined his partner and they drove away.

When Thomas went to the guest bedroom, normally reserved for visitors, he found Amy and Deanna asleep on the bed, Deanna snuggled into the crook of Amy's arm. He smiled at the sight, then went and moved the crib across the hallway and into the guest room as quietly as possible. Deanna murmured a little as he transferred her over, but he was thankful she didn't awaken. Then Thomas lay down beside Amy, pulling a comforter over them both, and finally managed to get back to sleep.

Later in the day, as Thomas was checking out the damage to the front of the parsonage, he turned around and happened to see someone walking through the pasture across the road.

Without even stopping to think, he called out to the person and started walking across his lawn and the road. The man on the other side of the fence stopped and turned toward him, then walked closer to the pasture fence. As Thomas approached, he saw that this was an older man, maybe fifty, stocky, with graying hair and a goatee to match.

"Reverend Wilson, isn't it? I don't think we've met, but I know your name from the church sign." The man stuck out his hand, and Thomas shook it as a matter of habit. "I'm Charles

Rothstein. I own this property. Did you need something?" The man looked at Thomas expectantly.

"Mr. Rothstein, it's very nice to meet you. I, um... well, I have a couple of questions for you, if you wouldn't mind answering them."

The older man's eyes narrowed a little. "This isn't one of those 'proselytizing' things, is it? I'm Jewish, Reverend, and I attend the synagogue in Pennington, Temple Beth Shalom. I don't need to be evangelized."

Thomas laughed and shook his head. "No, no... don't worry, I won't try to drag you into our church, though you are welcome to visit any time you wish. Actually, this is about the deer in your pasture, and some things that have been happening lately."

"Reverend, are the deer coming over the fence and eating from your garden? If they are, all I can say is 'Build a fence!'. I can't be responsible for their actions..." he began.

Thomas raised a hand and shook his head. "And it's not that, either. Actually, it is about some people who have been trying to spotlight the deer in your pasture at night."

The owner of the pasture stopped with his mouth hanging open. "What the... how would you know, anyway?"

"Mr. Rothstein, I know because three times in the last month I have been awakened from a sound sleep by the gunshots." The man opened his mouth to protest, but Thomas continued, "I realize that isn't your fault. But it isn't just the deer.

"Someone, some person, has been in the field with the deer, and I am afraid he or she will be shot by the poachers! They have no problem endangering the lives of others. Just last night they shot at my home, the parsonage there," and he pointed across the road at the parsonage. "They damaged the brick, as well as shooting out two security lights, with buckshot. My wife, my daughter and I were sleeping in the house at the time."

Mr. Rothstein's face registered shock now. "My God! Were any of you hurt?"

Thomas shook his head. "No, thank the Lord. But these people seem to have no worries about injuring anyone."

The other man frowned. "But you mentioned 'some person' being up here with the deer. What do you mean? I never come up here at night, and although I have seen deer in the field, I certainly haven't been able to get close to them!"

"Well, someone is able to do so. Mr. Rothstein, this may be hard to believe, but a couple of days ago, right at dusk, I saw someone standing up here with three or four deer, and that person appeared to be petting a large buck – or touching it, at any rate. It didn't run or seem fearful at all."

"That's hard to believe, Reverend! Are you sure about that?" Rothstein's voice was skeptical.

Thomas then told him about the first time he saw the mysterious person, and going up the next day to check for any sign, then finding the footprints. "I'm sorry if I was trespassing, Mr. Rothstein, but there wasn't a 'No Trespassing' or 'Posted' sign, and I was very curious," Thomas apologized.

"Reverend, don't worry about it. I understand. I don't think you would be up here doing anything illegal, anyway. And please call me Charles." He shook his head, frowning in puzzlement. "Someone up here, dancing around in the moonlight, and petting wild deer? For the life of me, I have no idea who that may have been!"

"Do you ever have people camping on the property?" Thomas asked.

Charles snorted. "Not that I am aware of. But that doesn't mean anything. Since I've sold off the beef cattle for this year, I don't get up here too often. And even when I did come up here, I didn't search the woods for campers – didn't think I needed to!"

"I don't know that this person was doing anything wrong, Charles," Thomas said. "I'm really more worried about what might happen to them if the poachers continue to shoot up into the field and woods at night. A high-powered rifle bullet carries a long way."

Charles nodded. "I understand. But if anyone is camping up there, and I don't do anything to stop it, and they do end up getting shot... well, I would feel somewhat responsible. I think I'll go to town today and buy some 'No Trespassing' signs and some more 'No Hunting' signs, and post them all along the fence and on a few of the trees." He shrugged. "It won't stop the poachers or any campers, certainly, but at least I will have warned them, and this unknown person, that I don't want them doing what they are doing."

"The police have said they are going to double up on the patrols by here, which I hope will help," Thomas offered.

Mr. Rothstein nodded and turned to go. "You'll forgive me, Reverend, but if I'm going to buy those signs and get them put up, I need to get on my way. It was nice meeting you." They shook hands, and Thomas headed back to the parsonage as Charles walked away to where Thomas now saw he had a Jeep parked near the pasture gate.

* * *

The next day after the morning service, Thomas was shaking hands and greeting people as they left the church. Amy walked up and touched his arm to get his attention. She was accompanied by a member of the youth group, Melanie Peterson.

"Melanie has agreed to be our babysitter Thursday night, Thomas," Amy said.

Thomas turned and smiled at the young girl. She was about 15, blonde-haired and pale-skinned, with large blue-gray eyes. Her parents were both descendants of Swedish immigrants to Wisconsin. They had moved to their present home from Wisconsin when Melanie was 12. They all still had a trace of the Wisconsin accent that crept into their conversation once in a while.

"Think you can handle Deanna, Melanie?" Thomas asked.

"Oh, for sure. I help out in the church nursery sometimes, don't ya know? I've seen Deanna a few times there, and she's always a very good baby. Not fussy at all." Melanie was very confident, which probably came from having four younger siblings she babysat all the time.

"Great! We're looking forward to seeing this play, and we appreciate you helping us out," Thomas told her.

She grinned, then excused herself to go and talk with some other members of the youth group.

Thomas, Amy and Deanna enjoyed a quiet lunch at home, followed up by phone calls to their respective parents. Thomas's parents lived in Texas, and Amy's lived in Virginia. The attendance was a little low at the evening service that day, but Thomas consoled himself with the knowledge that attendance fluctuates constantly.

As he and Amy were walking back to the parsonage that night, a police car cruised slowly by, and it flashed its lights at them in greeting. While it was cheering to see that the police were living up to what they promised, it was also an uneasy reminder of the possibility of more gunshots.

As Thomas looked up at the night sky, he wondered if he should replace the security lights, or if they would just draw more destructive gunfire from the poachers. That is when an idea occurred to him, and he couldn't wait to get into the house to verify its possibility.

Once inside the house, Thomas called Stan Bowman at his home.

"Pastor! Seems like I just left you at the church!" Stan joked. "What can I do for you?"

"Stan, don't you have a set of night vision binoculars or something like that?" Thomas asked.

"Well, it's only a monocular, but it is night vision, yes. Why do you ask?"

"I was thinking on the way back to the parsonage about ways to look at the poachers without attracting their gunshots with new security lights. I remembered you telling me about your night vision scope earlier this summer, and how much you enjoyed using it to watch the raccoons out at your place."

"So, you got the idea of possibly looking at the poachers with the night vision scope? Great idea!" Stan caught on immediately.

"Are you using the scope now? I mean, in the near future."

"No, and if I was, I'd still let you borrow it. Stopping those poachers is important, and as a legitimate hunter, I'm doubly anxious to stop them. When do you want the scope?" Stan asked.

"I can pick it up tomorrow, Stan. I don't expect them to come by again tonight, not after shooting the lights out last night." At least, I hope not, he thought.

Thomas was correct in his assumption. The night passed without any disturbance, and they all three slept serenely.

The next day, Thomas drove out to the building site for the new church, near the intersection of Highway 62 and Holly Creek Road. There, he met Simon Daniels, who had taken a strong interest in helping to manage the building of the church. While Simon was not a builder, his knowledge of the church's general way of operating, the members and their preferences, was helping the general contractor tailor the church building more closely to what the members of Holly Creek Christian Church would want and need.

"Mornin', pastor! How are you doin' today?" was Simon's cheery greeting. "Come out to see how we're comin' along with the sanctuary?"

"Simon, I know I can trust you to let me know of any problems. I just wanted to take a look. It's encouraging to see it taking shape, considering all the trouble we went through to get this project started!" Thomas went over and stood beside Simon, watching the electrical contractors running conduit and wires throughout the structure.

In a few minutes the general contractor came over with some questions about the location of microphone and speaker outlets, and he, Simon and Thomas walked around the rostrum area deciding where would be best. After that was settled, Thomas left to take care of his Monday visitation schedule.

As Thomas left the roughly graveled parking area around the church construction site, he glanced over the vehicles parked there. With a start, he hit the brakes and his minivan slid a couple of feet in the loose gravel. Eyes wide, he stared.

There was a beat-up, red pickup truck with the gun rack in the back window. It was the same one he followed briefly the other day, and that he suspected was the one the poachers used. He reached into his dash and brought out his memo pad. Yes, there was no doubt about it now: the first three license plate numbers were exactly the same as the ones he wrote down before. The scoped deer rifle was still in the rear window, too. The rest of the numbers were visible now, so he copied them down, too. And there was another hint: mounted on both sides of the truck cab were old-fashioned swivel spotlights like the ones found in police cars.

Thomas stopped his vehicle and reversed to park near the unfinished church. Once inside, he located Simon again and asked him to come outside to have a private discussion.

"Simon, remember I was telling you and the other men about how people have been trying to spotlight deer across the road from the parsonage?" he asked in a low voice.

Simon nodded. "Yep, I remember. And somebody said they came back and shot at the parsonage, though I didn't really believe somebody would be low enough to do that!"

"Well, that did happen, Simon," and Thomas told him all the details of that event.

"That's terrible! But my guess is, you didn't roll back in here just to tell me about that. What do you need from me, pastor?" Simon asked, a shrewd expression on his face.

"Each time I have been awakened by the gunshots, I have heard a loud roaring engine as it accelerated, then a pause like

33

the transmission took a second to catch up, followed by squealing tires and the sound of the car or truck leaving."

Simon nodded. "Slipping transmission – used to happen all the time with the Jeeps I worked on in Viet Nam."

"Exactly. Well, I was in town last week, and that truck over there," he pointed, "was beside me at a red light. It had a deer rifle with a scope hanging in the back window, just like it does now. When the light turned red, the driver tromped on the accelerator, and it sounded exactly like the vehicle used by the poachers, even down to the slipping transmission. I've turned in the license plate to the police, so they are checking on it. What I'd like you to do, Simon, is to keep your eyes and ears open around the guy that drives that truck, and see if he says or does anything suspicious." Thomas put his hand on Simon's shoulder. "Don't do anything dangerous, or anything like that. Just be observant, that's all. Do you mind doing that?"

Simon grinned. "Shoot, pastor, we make a great team. I don't mind one bit. I'll be careful, don't you worry." They shook hands, and Thomas left the building site. He was confident that if the driver of that truck bragged about spotlighting deer, Simon would hear about it.

Thomas proceeded to Stan Bowman's house, where the slender, lantern-jawed man was finishing raking his lawn. Thomas got out of his vehicle and said, "Looks like I got here just in time!"

Stan stopped, rake in his hand, a puzzled expression on his face. "Just in time? Pastor, I just finished the job!" Then his face split in a grin as Thomas laughed. "Oh! That's the point, is it?" He made a mock-threat of swinging the rake at Thomas as he came over.

Stan leaned the rake against the wall and invited Thomas into his brick ranch-style home. Stan shooed the beagle away that tried to jump all over him, and ushered Thomas into his den.

There, he opened a cabinet and pulled out a night-vision monocular.

"It works like a charm, pastor, even when there's hardly any light at all. If you can't see very well, though, there is a button here on the top that you can press in, that illuminates the area you are looking at with infrared. You and I can't see it, but it makes a BIG difference in what you see with the night vision scope."

"What sort of batteries do I need to use with it?" Thomas asked.

"It's one of the newer ones, so it's rechargeable. Here's the charger. In fact, if you are just sitting inside the house, just plug it in while you are using it, and it doesn't even use the batteries then at all." Stan handed Thomas the charger, and a sturdy plastic case to hold it all. "I sure hope it helps, pastor. Those folks must be crazy to shoot at a house where people are sleeping, 'specially with buckshot! They could kill someone!" Stan was visibly outraged.

"Well, I appreciate the loan of this, Stan, and I'll take good care of it." Thomas looked at the monocular a little more. "Hey, it looks like I could mount it on a tripod, too. Great!"

"I'll let you know how things go," Thomas said as they walked out to his vehicle. Like most men, Thomas liked gadgets, and he could hardly wait to see how well this one worked.

Chapter 4

The people that walked in darkness have seen a great light: they that dwell in the land of the shadow of death, upon them hath the light shined.

Isaiah 9:2

Thomas was very intrigued with the night vision scope he borrowed from Stan, and talked about it abstractedly all during the meal. A bemused Amy just shook her head as she cleaned up the dinner dishes while Thomas read through the operating manual for the device.

Thomas had already selected a spot in their front room. He moved a table and lamp from the window and arranged a chair behind his camera tripod, with the monocular perched atop it. He checked his range of vision, and he had a clear field of view. The little red light on the charger glowed encouragingly.

Thomas sat and played with little Deanna for a while, then gave her a bath while Amy relaxed for a bit with a book. But he kept looking out the living room windows, checking on the light level outside.

Soon, he judged it to be dark enough to test out the night vision monocular. Deanna had just drifted into a semi-asleep state, her thumb falling from her mouth, and Thomas eased her into her baby bed. Then, almost rubbing his hands together in satisfaction, he entered the living room and shut the door.

Just after he turned off all the lights and settled himself behind the scope, the door opened behind him and light poured in. He spun about in his chair, almost irritated, but smiled when he saw that Amy was bringing him a glass of milk and some sugar cookies. She sat them down on the floor beside his chair and leaned down to kiss his cheek. "There, honey... now you have milk and cookies to go with your toy!" And with a laugh she scampered from the room.

The remark about the "toy" notwithstanding, Thomas enjoyed the cookies as he played with the different settings and adjustments on the scope. He marveled at how clearly things stood out for him. The box hedges along the front of the lawn looked like large, dark blobs until he looked through the scope, and suddenly they had branches and leaves that were crisp and distinct.

The night was slightly overcast, with the moon occasionally peeping through breaks in the clouds. Even with this variance in the light, though, Thomas was pleased with the performance of the scope. This was going to help a lot, he thought.

Soon, as he was munching a cookie, he saw what he thought was movement in the field. Putting his eye to the scope, he scanned the area and refocused. Deer! There were two... no, four deer there on the gentle slope of the pasture. And he could see them very clearly. The switching of their tails, the lowering and raising of their heads to graze and look about, and the swiveling of their ears to catch any possible sound – these were all easily visible.

He got up and left the room to get Amy, so she could see. They both returned and he asked her to sit down in the chair he had just vacated. "You may have to adjust the focus for your eyes, honey," he said, indicating the focus ring.

Amy fiddled with the focus, and a muffled exclamation came from her. "Thomas! I thought you were teasing me, but this is very clear! It reminds me of those news images they have sometimes, where the police or the soldiers are leading an assault on a house at night." She moved the scope from left to right a little, then stopped suddenly and gasped.

"Thomas! I see your strange dancing person! Only... only he isn't dancing, he's just walking over toward the deer!" Her hushed voice held an edge of excitement.

Thomas was antsy to see, too, but he peered through the window instead. He could see a vague shape moving through the cloud-cast shadows, but in no way could he identify it as a person. Thomas looked at his watch. It was only about ten PM.

Amy stood up. "Here, honey – take a look. I think it's a guy, but that's just my intuition speaking."

Thomas quickly sat down and refocused the scope. As the walking figure came into sharper focus, Thomas realized Amy probably had it right. The person didn't move like a woman, nor did it have womanly curves. The hair was pretty short, too. "I think you're right, Amy!"

Thomas watched in amazement as the figure eased up to the deer who were grazing. One acted a little nervous, but the other three looked up, then unconcernedly went back to eating. There was no buck in the group tonight, only four does. Then, without any warning, a gunshot rang out. The four deer alerted, flipped up their starkly white tails and dashed over the top of the hill. The human figure turned and ran at a semi-crouch for the safety of the woods.

Thomas pulled his eye from the monocular eyepiece. There was not a single car or truck on the highway! He leaped to his feet, almost knocking over the tripod, and ran for the front door. He heard another gunshot as he opened the front door, and he thought he saw a flash of red-orange light from the woods on the opposite side of the field, away from where the figure had fled. Had the person been hit? Or was he gone to ground, trying to stay as low as possible to avoid being shot?

Quickly, Thomas dialed 9-1-1, and the dispatcher sent a police car to the scene. They must have been only a mile or two away, because it seemed like less than a minute had elapsed before they were pulling up in the drive, blue lights flashing. It was Officer Riesling again.

Amy and Thomas both made statements to the patrolman. Riesling was pointedly not trying to look skeptical about the figure in the field. He asked, "Are you both sure that the person who shot was not just shooting at the deer?"

Thomas shook his head, and replied in a firm voice, "Absolutely sure, officer. The deer scattered with the first shot, running back over the hill and out of sight. The second shot came when only the figure was in sight."

Riesling nodded, but still looked unconvinced. He took a bright handheld torch to make a quick search of the field. When he came back and told them he saw sign of the deer, but had not found any signs of a person – no blood, footprints or anything else. Although Riesling stayed there for about an hour, waiting for another possible disturbance, there were no more gunshots that night, and no more sightings of either the deer or the mysterious figure.

* * *

Thomas prayed fervently that night before going to sleep. Indeed, it was only the relief of tension by prayer that finally allowed him to achieve sleep. But when he woke the next morning, it was with a resolve to discover what was going on in that field across the road!

After the alarm clock went off at 7:00, Thomas had a quick fried egg sandwich. Then he dressed himself in jeans, sweatshirt and sneakers, and set off across the road to the field where the deer congregated. But this time he also took along a small digital camera he had been given as a Christmas present last year. If he found any evidence, he reasoned, he would photograph it before it became disturbed or destroyed.

The morning dew soon soaked his sneakers and the legs of his jeans, and the chill November air made him think twice about what he was doing. But then he remembered the frantically fleeing deer, and the unknown person, running to save his or her own life.

By now, Thomas had spent so much time looking at the field that he had a pretty good idea where the person was entering and leaving the woods. He headed for that area, keeping his eyes open for any clues he might see.

Thomas had the advantage of daylight, so he was not surprised that he found signs of the unknown person's passage into the woods, that Officer Riesling missed. He took quick photos of disturbed pine needles and scuff marks in the earth, then attempted to follow the trail into the forest.

The trail was easy to see for about thirty yards, but then it seemed the fleeing person had felt safe enough to walk with more care, and the signs of his passage disappeared. Thomas made a couple of circular searches radiating out from the last point of the visible trail, but there was no further sign. He took photos of the end of the trail and on his way back he took photos of the trail along the way.

Thomas called Detective Lamonde at the police department to tell him about the events of last night and the photos he had taken that day. But Eric wasn't in. The person Thomas spoke with said he wasn't expected to be in at all that day, as he had court appearances scheduled for the entire day. So, Thomas decided to drive out to the church building site again, and see if Simon had heard anything.

When Thomas arrived at the site, he quickly scanned the parked vehicles for the red pickup truck. But it wasn't there.

Thomas parked and went inside, and found Simon in conversation about the placement of urinals in the men's restroom.

"Now, we want at least one of them three urinals to be low enough for a man in a wheelchair," he was instructing the plumber. "We have about four folks who are handicapped, and in the next couple of years, prob'ly more!" Thomas grinned at Simon's manner – this was probably the man the other soldiers in the motor pool had seen when they went looking for Sergeant Daniels.

Simon turned around and saw Thomas standing there. "Oh, hello, pastor! Sorry, didn't know you was there!"

"No problem, Simon. Can we talk outside?" Thomas asked.

Simon nodded and followed him out into the parking area. Thomas gestured around. "The red pickup truck – it's not here today. Is the driver here in another vehicle?"

Simon shook his head. "Nope. I found out the driver's name. It's Lance Hoskins. He's a young feller, smart-mouthed but a hard worker. 'Bout nineteen, I reckon. He ain't been here today at all."

"Did you hear anything about the spotlighting?"

Again, the answer was no. "Sorry, pastor, but not a peep. I asked some of the fellers about hunting this year, how it's been goin' for 'em, that sort of thing." He snorted. "'Course, if I believed half the stories I heard, they's monster bucks out there that would tote a feller off – but for some reason even though they're huge, nobody seems to be able to hit 'em. I don't think I'd admit it if I couldn't hit a target that big!" He grinned, then returned to the subject.

41

"Nobody has said anything 'bout anybody spotlightin' any deer this year, although two fellers did say they knew about somebody who did it last year, and killed five deer!" The outrage was strong in Simon's voice. "I had to bite my tongue to stay quiet on that one!"

Thomas clapped Simon on the shoulder. "Thanks for controlling yourself, Simon. Wouldn't do for you to seem to be too strict about the law, if you want them to open up about someone who poaches deer that way."

"Did somebody try to shoot a deer last night?" Simon asked.

"I'm not really sure! That's the problem." And Thomas told Simon about the shots fired last night, how they didn't come from any vehicle, and how he went into the field this morning to try to find a trace of the strange figure.

Simon's eyes were wide, but there was a calculating look on his face. "You were lookin' at the field when the shots were fired, right, pastor?"

Thomas nodded.

"Did you see a muzzle flash? A reddish-orange light?"

Thomas, startled, realized that he had, but in the excitement of the moment had forgotten all about it. "Yes, Simon, I did!"

"Well, that's the next place I'd look, pastor – the place where you saw the muzzle flash. Or more likely, the place the police ought to be lookin'."

Thomas left a little while afterward, and on the way home, he mentally beat himself over the head for not bringing this to the attention of Officer Riesling the night before. When he arrived home, he called the police station and asked if Officer Riesling was in. By chance, he was, working on some reports. Thomas was patched through to his phone.

"Reverend Wilson? What can I do for you, sir?" asked Riesling.

"I believe I forgot an important detail last night, officer. I can't remember. Did I tell you about the muzzle flash I saw when the second shot was fired?"

"No, sir, you didn't. Where did you see the muzzle flash?" Riesling asked.

Thomas gave a description of the field, and the approximate location of the muzzle flash relative to the landmarks there. Riesling thanked him, and said someone would go out and investigate that area as soon as possible.

That night, Thomas led Bible study for about 60 people in the sanctuary. His topic was taken from the Epistle of James, and was about expressing one's faith through action, not just words. As he was praying the closing prayer, there was a faint sound of thunder, and by the time people were leaving the church to go home, a steady rain was falling.

Melanie Anderson approached them before leaving the church. "You still need me for tomorrow night, right?" she asked.

"Yes, we do. Has anything come up so you can't babysit for us, Melanie?" Amy asked.

"Oh, no way! I just wanted to check, make sure you still needed me." The girl smiled and waved goodbye as she dashed out to her parents' waiting car, its windshield wipers making swooshing sounds in the increasing downpour.

Amy looked out the door, then at blanket-wrapped Deanna in her arms. Thomas read her look, grabbed one of the large golf umbrellas they kept in the church foyer for just such emergencies, and they hurried off to the parsonage after locking up.

The rain continued throughout the night, and into the next morning. As Thomas stood looking out into the rain and mist, sipping his morning coffee, he decided that any search for clues near where the muzzle flash was seen would likely be fruitless.

But later that day, a little after lunch, it stopped raining and soon a police car drove up to their driveway. The policeman and Thomas walked across the road and over to where Thomas remembered seeing the muzzle flash. The grass and the soil beneath were sodden, and Thomas despaired of finding any traces.

He tried to help with the search at first, but a glance from the officer let him know he should just stay back out of the way. After about 15 minutes, Thomas was ready to call it quits, but the policeman, whose name was Farrell, bent over and retrieved something glistening with the tip of his pen. He turned around and walked over to Thomas, a grin on his face.

"This is a .30-06 cartridge, reverend. Now, it looks pretty new, but the really telling thing is the scent. Here, sniff," and he held the shell casing out for Thomas to smell.

He did, and immediately was struck by the scent of burned gunpowder. "That's freshly fired, or at least fairly fresh," he said.

Officer Farrell nodded. "That's what I say, too, sir." He put the casing into a small plastic bag, and returned to searching, but found nothing else. They slogged back to the parsonage, and as the officer left he assured Thomas they would check the casing for fingerprints, if there were any to be had after it had been in the mud and rain.

That success made Thomas eager to track down the mysterious figure. Since it was no longer raining, Thomas put his boots on again, and slipped across the road. He went directly to where he found the original trail into the woods, and started following it once more. It was easier now that he had been there before.

When he got to the point where the trail ended, he stood and looked around himself. Where would a person go from here? South would take them deeper into Mr. Rothstein's property, and up a long sloping hill.

North would take them back to the main thoroughfare, Holly Creek Road. That probably wouldn't be a good choice, either. But Thomas knew there was a small side road that went south from Holly Creek Road about 100 yards further west, and it was seldom traveled, except by the two families who lived out at the end of it.

So, Thomas set his face westward and plodded on through the wet brush. Dripping pine branches unloaded their cargo of water on his head and down his back, and his shirt soon became soaked, despite the jacket he was wearing. But there in front of him, he could see a little light where the forest was clearing.

Thomas emerged from the woods about ten yards from a barbed-wire fence. He slipped between the strands of barbed wire, and caught his jacket as he did so, hearing a small ripping sound. Amy wouldn't be happy about that!

He could see one place where it appeared a car had parked on the side of the road several times – or at least enough times to leave the grass compressed flat. He looked all around the area. He couldn't see any other clues, though. Looking at his watch, he realized with a start that he needed to head back home, as they had plans to go to dinner before the play tonight.

He returned to the fence, and bent to spread the strands so he could slide between them. As he did so, he saw something shining, catching the few rays of sunlight that were filtering through the hazy sky. He reached down, and picked up a driver's license.

The license was that of a young man named Eddie Kusack. A smiling, dark-haired young man looked up at Thomas from the bad license picture. From his birthday on the license, the young man was 17 years old.

Thomas almost shouted "hallelujah!" right there. Persistence pays off, he thought. Tucking the license into this pocket, Thomas hurried back to the parsonage. He'd tell Detective Lamonde about it tomorrow.

As Thomas came out of the woods and into the pasture, he saw Mr. Rothstein just getting out of his jeep, inside the fence. He waved at the older man, but did not receive such a friendly greeting in return.

"Mr. Wilson, what are you doing in my field again?" the man said, sounding a little angry. "I told you I was getting some 'No Trespassing' signs and putting them up, didn't I?"

Thomas was taken aback. "Well, yes sir, you did. But you also said you knew I wouldn't be doing anything illegal up here, too. Besides," and he motioned, "there aren't any signs up, except for 'No Hunting,' and I haven't been hunting... well, not for deer, anyway.

"But I did find something very interesting!" Thomas announced and pulled the license from his pocket to show it to Mr. Rothstein. He was puzzled by the look of shock on Rothstein's face just then, but the man's face cleared, as he took the driver's license and looked at it.

"Hmmm. Eddie Kusack." He studied the picture for a few moments, then shook his head and handed it back to Thomas. "Where did you find this, anyway?"

Thomas explained how he had discovered where the boy must have parked his car and gone through the fence. "But I'm still puzzled by his actions! Why was he here late at night, and how was he so friendly with the deer?" Thomas asked in a wondering voice. "Do you know the boy?" he asked Rothstein, gesturing with the license.

"Me? No, I don't think so, and I don't know why he'd be here on my land, either."

"Do you have any idea why someone would be shooting at him?"

Rothstein's head came up very suddenly, and he went pale. "Shooting at him? Why, did someone shoot at him? When?"

Thomas told him briefly about the nighttime shooting, realizing by the dimming light that he was approaching being late. "Mr. Rothstein, I do apologize if I offended you by coming up here like this, but the thing has been pressing on my mind. Now that I've found this, though, I don't think I will need to be up here again." He looked at his watch. "And I hate to rush, but my wife and I have a commitment tonight, and I have to go."

"Not a worry, you go ahead. Listen, though, if you need to come up here again, do me a favor and call me before you do, OK? It would make me feel better about the whole thing. Here's my card, with my home and my mobile phone numbers on it." Rothstein handed him a business card, and Thomas shoved it into his pocket without even looking at it.

"Certainly will, Charles. Thanks!" Thomas hurried back home, and walked quickly past a toe-tapping Amy to take a quick shower and dress in a dark suit. When he came out, Melanie was already there, and Amy was giving her the short tour, showing her where the phone numbers were, the soda and

47

chips, and all the necessary things that new parents are concerned about the first time a babysitter keeps their child.

Melanie herded them both toward the door. "Sister Wilson, you two are going to be late! Deanna is a sweet baby, and I'm sure we won't have any troubles." Thomas thanked Melanie again, and assured her they would be back by 11:00 or so.

They managed to relax for a little while at a little Greek restaurant Amy liked – she had thought far enough ahead to call and make reservations. While they were there, Thomas showed her the driver's license he found, how he found it and about showing it to Mr. Rothstein.

"Mr. Rothstein acted very strange about my being there, though. He seemed upset about it," Thomas said over baklava at the end of the meal.

"Well, after all, he has people shooting at his deer, he had this strange unknown figure, who we now think is Eddie Kusack, and even had someone shooting at the figure as well! I guess he would be a little anxious about people in the field," Amy said.

Thomas stopped chewing for a moment, looking thoughtful, then swallowed. "You know, that's funny, too. When I told him about someone shooting at the mystery person he acted really shocked – he went white to the lips!"

"As for Mr. Rothstein being upset," Amy shook her head, "do you blame him? I mean, having someone shot on your property would be a terrible thing, especially if they were killed! Even if you had no compassion at all, the legal side of it and the publicity could be terrible."

"I suppose so," Thomas said slowly, seeing in his mind the face of the surprised and almost frightened Mr. Rothstein. Thomas looked up as the check arrived. Thomas paid the check, and he and Amy left for the play at Temple Beth Shalom.

As Larry promised, two tickets were waiting for them in an envelope marked "Thomas and Amy Wilson". He took the tickets, acquired two playbills, and entered the auditorium. There were two policeman in uniform standing near the entrances. Amy looked at them curiously as the passed.

"What is the reason for the policemen?" she whispered to Thomas.

"Lots of schools hire off-duty policemen now for events – just in case there is any sort of problem. Sad that it's necessary, but it helps to cover the school for liabilities," Thomas answered in a similar whisper.

They were running a little late, so there wasn't much time to chat. Within minutes, the house lights dimmed, and the play began.

The stage looked much more like a 1940's English sitting room now, and the costumes were great, even if the young "secretary" seemed to be a bit overdressed for the occasion. It was obvious the students had worked on their parts tirelessly, because there were no stumbles or pauses Thomas could detect.

The first act was approaching its climax now, and the young man playing the judge finished cross-examining everyone in the room. The characters were all discussing how they could get off the island, since there was no boat. But one of the actors, wearing a fake mustache, stood up and declared that it was unsporting to leave without figuring out the mystery.

He held up a glass of the "whiskey" as he had during practice when Thomas had been there before. "I'm all for crime," he declaimed. "Here's to it!" He drank it down at a swallow, clutched at his throat, gasping, and fell to the floor.

Thomas leaned over to Amy and said, "He's much better this time. When I saw him in rehearsal, he was flopping around like a landed fish when he died!" Amy giggled, then returned her attention to the play.

Esther Meyer, playing Emily Brent, was just moving forward and center on the stage, with a little broken figurine in her hands. "Look, here's one of the little Indians from the mantle, broken!" The curtain fell then, and the house lights came up. There was applause from the audience, and many people started to get up, as there was to be a fifteen-minute intermission at this point.

But a scream from the stage grabbed everyone's attention, and the chattered conversations died away. The curtains were thrown apart and the director dashed out, her hair awry.

"My God! Someone call an ambulance," she yelled in a hoarse voice, strangled with panic. "Eddie really is dead! He's dead!"

Chapter 5

For every kind of beasts, and of birds, and of serpents, and of things in the sea, is tamed, and hath been tamed of mankind: But the tongue can no man tame; it is an unruly evil, full of deadly poison.
James 3:7,8

Two or three people near Thomas and Amy laughed, thinking this was all part of the play. But as the woman continued to scream and plead for help, they stopped laughing. Larry Meyer worked his way through the crowd and pushed by Thomas, obviously agitated.

Thomas followed in Larry's wake after asking Amy to stay where she was. When Larry was a few feet from the side stage door, it burst open and several students poured out, some of them in costume. Esther was among them.

"Daddy! Oh, Daddy, Eddie is..." and she collapsed into her father's arms, sobbing. Larry embraced her tightly, trying to comfort her. Thomas didn't want to intrude on them, but soon someone else arrived who had no such hesitation.

A young man almost ran by Thomas, paused a moment to look at Larry and Esther, and then advanced more slowly. He put a hand on each of their shoulders. Thomas moved a little closer.

The young man was leaning down to put his face by Esther's speaking in a very low voice. But Esther turned her head away with another gulping sob, and Larry said something to the young man. He took a short step back, but kept his hands on both their shoulders.

"Mr. Meyer, I was only trying to..." he began.

"Brian, never mind what you were trying to do! Esther doesn't want to see or hear you right now, so go away!" Larry kept his voice controlled and low, but it was obvious he was in no mood

51

to tolerate this person's intrusion into the moment. Thomas went forward and put his hand on Brian's shoulder.

"Brian, Mr. Meyer and his daughter need to be left alone right now," Thomas said in a quiet voice. The young man whirled, his face tightening and his green eyes flaring wide.

"Just who are you, and why are you butting in here, anyway?" Brian snarled. "This is none of your business!"

Thomas leaned in closer and gripped Brian's arm just above the elbow. He spoke directly into Brian's ear, in a soft voice no one else could hear. "Brian, Larry is my good friend, and he wants you to leave him and his daughter alone. Now, you can do it quietly like a gentleman, or I can walk you out of here and into the hands of those policemen in the lobby. Which is it?"

The young man's eyes narrowed and he jerked his hand away from Thomas's grip. He turned and pushed rudely through the crowd, looking back once or twice with a very fierce expression. Thomas shook his head, then returned his attention to Larry and Esther.

"Larry, is there anything I can do to help?" he asked.

"I think you just did," Larry said, gently moving his daughter's hair back from her face. "That guy is Esther's ex-boyfriend. He used to go to school here, but he graduated here last year." Larry snorted. "His parents are not members of the synagogue. They paid his tuition, though, so he came here. It's a very good school, with a great reputation," he explained.

"I guess that explains why he thought he could just push in and speak to Esther, then," Thomas observed. "Pretty rude of him not to leave when asked, though."

"He's been trying to get back together with Esther for about four months, now. But she's been dating Eddie Kusack," and he squeezed Esther tighter, as she sobbed into his chest again. "So, she just isn't interested in Brian any more."

Thomas's eyes widened. "I'm sorry, but did you say Eddie Kusack?" he asked.

Larry frowned, then nodded. "Yes, Eddie. The boy who was... well, you know, the one on the stage – with the mustache." He gestured to his sobbing daughter, and they all stood aside to allow paramedics to get through the crowd with a gurney, headed for the stage area.

"Larry, I'm sorry, I'm not being obtuse, but it's the strangest thing. Eddie Kusack is the name of the boy who – the boy the paramedics are here to see?" Thomas swallowed hard as he asked.

Larry frowned at Thomas's apparent lack of understanding. "Yes, Thomas – that was Eddie Kusack! Why do you ask?"

"Larry, this is not a good time, but I'll tell you more later, OK? It's just that I believe I found Eddie's driver's license in the weeds of a ditch near the church!" Thomas didn't know what else to say.

Esther raised her tear-stained face, smeared makeup painting strange patterns on her cheeks. "You found his license? He's been saying he lost it about three days ago, and he wasn't sure where!" She struggled with the words. "Where did you say you found his license?" Esther sounded puzzled.

"In the weeds of a ditch, not far from my church, Esther. I have the license at home. I had no idea he attended school here, or that he was even in the play, else I would have brought the license here to give to him..." Thomas trailed off, as the paramedics came back through the auditorium, carrying Eddie's body on the gurney. They had his face covered with

53

the sheet, and Esther broke into another storm of sobs, crushing her face against her father's chest.

The paramedics were closely followed by a group of solemn and crying student actors, all looking rather stunned. The director was leaning on an older, gray-haired woman, and seemed to almost fall once or twice.

After they passed, Thomas, Larry and Esther started back up the aisle of the auditorium. The crowd was thinning now, shock lining everyone's face. As they approached Amy, she stepped out into the aisle and put her hand on Esther's shoulder. Esther looked up to see who it was, and turned toward Amy, stricken. Amy put her arm around Esther, and they sat down together there in the auditorium seats.

"I'm glad you and Amy are here," Larry murmured as they walked a few feet away. "Esther's mother couldn't be here because she's at a conference in Nashville. She gets back tomorrow, but I'm sure Esther needs a female figure right now, too."

Thomas looked at Amy and Esther, and saw that Amy was talking in a subdued tone to Esther, and that the girl was nodding as she wiped her tears. "Amy has a way of reaching people who are hurting," Thomas said. "It's one of her gifts from God."

Larry nodded, then turned to look directly into Thomas's face. "Now, what is this about Eddie's driver's license, and why was it so difficult to say?"

Thomas shook his head. "Not difficult to say, only involved. Briefly, though, there has been someone in the field across the road from the parsonage. He has been there at night a few times. Well, the other night while I watched this unknown person in the field, someone shot at them."

Larry was startled. "What do you mean? By accident, like a hunting accident?"

"No, I think it was on purpose," Thomas said. "The police came out and investigated a little. They found an empty rifle cartridge of a caliber used to hunt big game, like deer, but these shots were fired at the person in the field.

"Later, when I went back into the field, I followed the person's trail through the woods on the opposite side. It came out near a fence beside a road. It looked like a car had been parked there a few times, and I found a driver's license for Eddie Kusack in the weeds of the ditch, near the barbed-wire fence." He shrugged. "It could have fallen from his shirt pocket as he bent to go through the fence strands."

Larry's expression became more and more puzzled as Thomas told him of the license and how he found it. "You're leaving out some details, Thomas, you must be. It doesn't make sense!"

With a sigh, Thomas said, "Well, even with the details it doesn't make a lot of sense." He looked past Larry at Amy and Esther. They both had stood up and were hugging each other. "I think Esther may be ready to go, Larry. Tell you what – why don't we have lunch together tomorrow. I'll tell you all about what has been going on, and I'll bring the license with me..." Thomas stopped. "No, wait a minute. I can let you see it, but with all that has happened, I think I should turn it in to the police. It's evidence."

Larry frowned. "Evidence?"

"Yes, evidence. We don't think Eddie died a natural death tonight, do we?" Larry had a bleak expression on his face as he shook his head. "Well," Thomas said, "someone shot at him the other night. One attempted murder, and one successful murder. I think that would make it evidence, don't you?"

55

Esther walked up and put her arm through her father's arm just then, so Larry just had to content himself with "You're right. Lunch tomorrow, then. 12:30 alright?"

Thomas nodded. "That's fine. I'll come by the pharmacy and we can walk up to the deli on the corner." He reached out and took Esther's hand. "I'll be praying for you, and for Eddie, Esther."

On the way home from the synagogue, both Amy and Thomas were silent at first. They reached out and took each other's hand at each red light, though, and it was evident that tonight's events shocked them both. Finally Amy broke the silence.

"Esther is such a sweet girl, Thomas. This is terrible for her, and I know it will be a terrible shock for Eddie's parents, too, when they find out."

Thomas glanced at her, puzzled. "When they find out? Why wouldn't they know tonight?"

"They are on a trip to the Cayman's right now. They've been gone for two weeks, but they're supposed to be back on Saturday, so they were going to see the last performance of the play." She sighed. "I don't know which would be the bigger shock – having someone contact you while you are away like that and let you know your child has been killed, or to arrive home and find out then." She shuddered. "Thomas, tell me that will never happen to us!"

"I pray God it never will!" he said fervently.

"Eddie was a very remarkable young man, according to Esther. He was a vegetarian – didn't believe in eating meat, thought it was both cruel and a terrible waste of resources to raise corn to feed cattle, when the same amount of corn could feed three or four times the number of people as the cattle would.

"She said he convinced her not to eat meat, either, but that it was hard since she liked burgers so much. And he was very much an anti-hunter. Several of the teenage boys around the school gave him a hard time over that. You now how big hunting is around here!"

Thomas almost ran off the road as he looked at Amy. "Amy, did Esther tell you Eddie's last name?"

Amy shook her head, puzzled. "No, it didn't come up. Why?"

"His name is Eddie Kusack," Thomas said, with emphasis on the last name.

"So? Am I supposed to know..." and suddenly Amy stopped, with her hand to her mouth. "Oh, my Lord! Do you mean, the name on the driver's license you found?"

"Yes! That name. And," Thomas continued, "it all fits! If Eddie is, or was, a confirmed anti-hunter, it wouldn't be out of character for him to go into the field. He could scare the deer when the poachers drove up and started shining the light around."

"But so late at night! He has been out there – wait! His parents have been gone to the Cayman Islands for the last two weeks. That would have given him the freedom to roam at night as he wished," Amy said. "He could have sat out there in the woods and waited, and then when the poachers showed up, he could yell or do something else to frighten the deer."

"Maybe jump up and down, waving his arms like a maniac?" Thomas suggested.

They were both silent for a while, absorbing all this. Then Amy asked, "Did they say what killed Eddie?"

"Not that I heard. They probably don't know yet. They'll have to do an autopsy. But I'm guessing that, if he WAS killed, it was poison," Thomas stated.

"Why do you say that?"

"Well, nobody said anything about something falling on him, or his bleeding or anything like that. Remember? The director yelled out, 'Eddie is really dead!' I figure when the curtain came down, they couldn't get him up from the floor. They checked, and he was dead, not acting. That's why I think it was poison."

"That's horrible, Thomas! What a terrible thing, and how dangerous! Any of those kids could have been poisoned by that drink of his!" Amy was aghast at the possibilities. "Oh, and Thomas! I remember how you said how much better his death scene was tonight than when you saw him the first time!" Her voice was shaky, and Thomas reached out to squeeze her hand.

"I know, honey, I know. I've been reproaching myself for saying that, ever since I knew he was dead."

"Did you tell Larry all about the deer, the poachers, and Eddie Kusack being in the pasture?"

"No, but I'm having lunch with him tomorrow, and I'll fill him in then. I'll show him Eddie's driver's license, and then I'll take it by the police station. They will probably want it for evidence."

They arrived at the parsonage a few minutes later, and Melanie met them at the door with a good report for the night. "Oh, no problems, Sister Wilson. Deanna took her last bottle, and I read her 'Good Night Moon Room'. While I was reading it to her, she just fell asleep and I've been watching TV since then."

She frowned. "But you are home way early! I didn't expect you for another hour and a half. Is anything wrong?"

Amy explained about the play, and how one of the actors died during the first act. Melanie's eyes grew round as golf balls, and she covered her mouth with her hands. When Amy told her who it was that died, she gasped. "The anti-hunting guy!" she said in a rush.

Thomas turned and looked at her. "Did you know Eddie Kusack, Melanie?"

She shook her head, her blonde hair swirling around her face. "No, I really didn't, but I remember the boys at my school talking about him. They thought he was a real weirdo because he was downtown the day before Halloween handing out flyers that said deer hunting was inhumane and barbaric! One of them said a guy came by while he was handing them out, and got so mad he took all Eddie's flyers and threw them in a dumpster. They almost got in a fight!"

"Do you know who threw his flyers in the dumpster, Melanie?" Thomas asked.

She shrugged, an apologetic expression on her face. "I don't know, pastor. I'm sorry."

"Well, that's OK. Want one of us to take you home?" Thomas asked.

"No, my mom said to just call her when I needed to come home." She fidgeted a little. "Ummm... I do need to get paid, though." She looked embarassed.

"Oh, Melanie, I'm sorry! You call your mom, and I'll get my purse," Amy exclaimed.

Melanie got off the phone with her mother, and Amy handed her the money. Melanie looked at it and said, "This is too much, Sister Wilson. I only babysat for two and a half hours."

"We agreed for four hours, Melanie, and it's not your fault the evening was cut short. So, you get paid for four hours. It's only fair," Amy said firmly, pushing the offered money back into Melanie's hand. Then her mother pulled up in the driveway and flashed her headlights. Melanie said "Thanks again," and left, waving goodbye.

Amy and Thomas went into the living room and sat down together. The television was still on, and Thomas turned it off with the remote. Almost simultaneously, the two of them asked each other, "How do you...?", then they stopped.

Thomas started again. "So, you are wondering how and why Eddie was poisoned, too?" Amy nodded. "It's nice that our minds follow the same paths sometimes, but it's also too bad that one of us can't answer that question for the other!" Thomas said in a sad voice.

"I know," Amy said. Her face was strained, and her eyes reddened from crying along with Esther as she comforted her. Thomas reached out and touched her shoulder.

"Honey, we have to put this in God's hands," Thomas said. "We said we would be praying for both Eddie and Esther, and I think we could use the reassurance of prayer for ourselves, as well." He took both her hands in his, and they prayed together for the Meyer family, for Esther and Eddie, and for Eddie's parents, that God would give them peace and understanding. They also prayed for the police investigating the murder, that they would be led to the right clues to discover the culprit and stop them from doing any further harm.

Amy wiped her eyes again, and took in a deep, shuddering breath. "You know, Thomas, outside of a hospital room or bedroom where I was attending the final moments of a friend or church member, I've never seen anyone die before." Her voice had a rough, uneven quality as she spoke. "But tonight, I saw a young man with so many years ahead, suddenly cut down because of the evil of another person, and it sickens me!

She looked down at her hands, which were folding and refolding a tissue. "And I'm angry, Thomas. I can't believe how angry I am! It was bad enough when those people killed Roger Henderson, but at least he had lived a full and productive life. Here was a young man, obviously with high ideals, who was cut down before he had a chance to fulfill his plans for life." Tears dropped down onto her lap.

"I know we're supposed to turn these things over to God, and I know we just prayed, but..." she swallowed hard, and continued, "all I can think about is that in a few years, Deanna is going to be that age, and what would I have done, if that had been her falling down dead on that stage tonight?"

Thomas slid closer to her and put his arms around her, feeling her body shaking slightly as she cried. He just held her like that for a little while, then with soft words of comfort, he helped her up and into the bedroom, where she lay down on the bed. He picked up little Deanna, still sleeping, and placed her in the crook of Amy's arm, then lay down beside them both. Both he and Amy fell asleep while he was stroking her hair.

But Thomas's sleep was anything but peaceful at first. He dreamed of being shot at while pursuing deer through a forest, and of being so tired and thirsty, then finding a glass of water in the woods but being afraid to drink it, in case it was poisoned. Eventually, though, his nightmares ceased, and he slept more easily.

Chapter 6

But I say unto you, Love your enemies, bless them that curse you, do good to them that hate you, and pray for them which despitefully use you, and persecute you; That ye may be the children of your Father which is in heaven: for he maketh his sun to rise on the evil and on the good, and sendeth rain on the just and on the unjust.

Matthew 5:44,45

Friday morning saw a foggy dawn, and a somewhat foggy outlook for Thomas. His sleep had not been as restful as he wanted. Little Deanna had been very cooperative, however, not asking for her normal middle-of-the-night feeding, although she was twice as hungry for breakfast.

Thomas walked over to the church early that morning, to study and pray as was his practice on Friday mornings. His prayers today were very focused, for the events of the past few days made him mindful of the attacks that came upon everyone, Christian and non-Christian alike. He was firmly convinced that Christians had no monopoly upon either the blessings of God or the attacks of the Devil. All suffered, and all were blessed. It was up to the individual to decide how to deal with what happened, and whether to blame God or to look for constructive ways to use God's blessings to defeat evil.

In fact, this became the subject for his sermon the following Sunday, as he meditated. And as he was studying, coming up with homiletical references, he looked at the clock on his desk. To his surprise, it was already after eleven o'clock, so he quickly gathered his notes together in a neat pile, and went to the parsonage to get ready to meet Larry Meyer for lunch.

Larry was waiting just inside the door to the pharmacy when Thomas arrived, so he came out and met Thomas on the sidewalk. The moist fog of the morning was almost dissipated, so they walked to Schwartzkopf's Delicatessen.

"How is Esther doing, Larry?" Thomas asked as they passed others bundled in jackets and overcoats against the November chill.

"She's doing better, but obviously it will take some time. I had no idea she was so smitten with this boy, Eddie." He sighed. "Thomas, I know you don't have one this age yet, but remember – it's important to get to know how they feel about their latest love interest, even if they don't seem to want to tell you! And it will happen with Deanna. When you and Amy brought her by the pharmacy the very first time, I could look at her and see that she will grow up into a beautiful young lady!"

"Thanks, Larry. When will Sharon get back from the conference in Nashville?" Thomas asked.

"Her plane arrives at the airport at 3:30, so she should be home by 5:00 or 5:30," Larry replied. "I called her and gave her a heads-up about what happened, and she was very upset, too. She knew more about how attached Esther was to Eddie, than I did. But I suppose it's normal for the mother to know more about those things."

Thomas nodded as he opened the door to the deli and they both entered. There were only a few small tables, as most people came for take-out sandwiches. Larry and Thomas were lucky to find one at the back, farther away from everyone, and they draped their coats over the chairs to claim it while making their orders at the counter.

After about half the corned-beef sandwiches and potato salad were consumed, Thomas began telling Larry about the deer, the poachers, the shots fired at the parsonage and the shots fired at the mysterious figure in the field.

Larry wasn't surprised at the poaching – after all, he grew up in the area and knew how important getting a big rack was to some people. But the idea of shooting at the house to destroy the security lights, and then someone shooting at Eddie (for they both agreed that it must have been Eddie), outraged him.

"And the police, what are they doing, Thomas? Are they digging into this?" Larry asked, attacking his potato salad as though it were the offending poacher.

"At first they weren't too excited by the poaching, because of this spate of break-ins that has happened. But when the poachers shot at the house with the buckshot, that got the attention of the police. They doubled the patrols by the house, and have been out to investigate."

"What about this figure in the field? Do they know it was Eddie?"

Thomas shook his head. "Not yet. I'm going to take the driver's license by there today. And that reminds me," he said, taking the license from his shirt pocket. "Is this Eddie?"

Larry took the laminated card from Thomas and it was as though a cloud passed over his face. He nodded, and handed it back to Thomas. "Yes, that's Eddie. He has been to the house several times. It doesn't look much like the boy you saw at the play because his hair is longer in the license picture, but that's him."

Thomas tucked the license away and was silent for a moment. He used a bite of sandwich to delay while he thought of how to phrase the question.

"Larry, how well did you know Eddie?"

Larry looked at Thomas, frowning a little. "Well, Thomas, how well does any father know the boy who is dating his teenage daughter?" He gave a humorless chuckle. "They seem to feel it necessary to hide all but the most necessary information. But last night, Esther sat up for a long time, telling me about Eddie." He sighed. "I guess she needed to talk about him; it helped her to clear her mind.

"She told me a lot about his ideology, a lot more about his feelings about what was humane and what was not. He was, according to her, a big stickler for human rights as well as animal rights. His family only moved to the area two years ago, you know? Before that, they lived in Massachusetts, and political activism is a big thing there."

"So he had been involved in protests, getting petitions signed, that sort of thing?" Thomas asked.

"Yeah, that sort of thing. He participated in an anti-fur protest when he was only fourteen, and worked all summer two years ago mowing lawns to save the money and send it to Greenpeace to help in their work to stop the hunters from slaughtering harp seals." Larry grinned. "You know how we Jews are – always rooting for the underdog."

Thomas laughed. "So, he was an animal lover, then." Larry nodded as he chewed his sandwich. "Do you think that he had any sort of special, well, affinity with animals?"

Larry frowned. "You mean, like that crazy TV show where the guy talks to animals telepathically?"

"No, nothing like that. But this person who was in the field was very, very close to the wild deer. In fact, one night it even looked like he was petting a large buck." Thomas watched for a reaction, and wasn't disappointed.

"Oy! Petting a buck deer? In November, during the rut? Come on, Thomas, what are you thinking? Did you actually SEE this?" Larry's face and voice showed his skepticism.

"Well, I saw what certainly appeared to be someone touching a deer's back, as he stood beside it." Thomas rescued himself from having to say more than that by filling his mouth with food.

Larry stared out the window for a few moments. "You know, that sounds crazy to me, but Esther did say that she was with Eddie at the park one day, and the squirrels were coming right up to him and taking peanuts out of his hand. She tried and tried, but they wouldn't get within a couple of yards of her." He shrugged. "Maybe it's because he doesn't eat meat. I've heard it said that people who eat meat have a different smell to their sweat, to their skin, than total vegetarians – at least a different smell that animals can sense. But to pet a wild deer? I don't know, Thomas." Larry shook his head and continued.

"Thomas, who do you think was shooting at Eddie that night? I mean, sure trespassing is a bad thing, but this land was not even posted, from what you tell me. Could it have been the owner?"

"Charles Rothstein? I don't think so. He seemed very concerned about anyone being there, but more about them getting shot by accident than about his land being trespassed on."

Larry looked startled. "Charlie Rothstein owns that field? I had no idea! He goes to my synagogue. Well, he doesn't attend regularly," Larry corrected, "but he's on the membership rolls. In fact, he was at the play Thursday night."

Now it was Thomas's turn to be surprised. "Really? I didn't see him there. Where was he sitting?"

"I saw him early, about thirty minutes before the curtain went up. He was leaving the men's room as I went in, and I noticed he headed toward the balcony stairs, so I assume he sat up there," Larry said.

"Why were you so startled to know he owns the field, Larry?"

Larry shrugged. "I just don't think of him as the 'farming sort', I guess. He owns a couple of businesses in the area – four, now that I think about it; two of them in Pennington and the other two are in Dixon. One in Pennington is a specialty shop for people who like to dress up their cars. They sell expensive add-ons, and do custom work like chrome, silver and even gold plating for rims, trim, etc. I think the other one is a sporting goods store or something like that."

Thomas's eyes widened. "Gold-plated rims? That has to be expensive!"

"Well, it's not something I would do to my Mustang, even though it is a classic! But Charles does a booming business, or so I've heard."

Thomas washed down his last bite, and sat looking at the styrofoam cup in his hand. "Larry, have you heard what happened to Eddie, anyway? I know we were theorizing last night, but have you heard anything definite?"

Larry just sat looking down at his food for a few seconds, then pushed back the remaining bit of his sandwich before answering, "Thomas, I wondered about that half the night. If he wasn't acting when he fell down to the floor, he had all the symptoms of a poison like cyanide. Cyanide poisoning burns the mucous membranes of the mouth and throat, causing the victim not to be able to breathe. In a strong enough concentration and in the right form, like sodium cyanide or potassium cyanide, it is very quickly fatal. But have I heard anything official? No."

Thomas sighed. "Our prayers will be with his family. Have they been told?"

Larry nodded. "Yes, the rabbi at the synagogue called them last night and informed them as gently as possible. He said they were beside themselves, but couldn't arrange a flight back until today. They should arrive late this afternoon."

"When will the funeral be held?"

"That depends on the findings of the autopsy. They have to hold one, you know, in a case like this. It's a good thing we are Reform, not Orthodox, or they might have a problem getting permission." Larry took a deep breath. "But I am sure the parents will want to know exactly what caused Eddie's death, and will want to do everything they can to find Eddie's killer."

"You're sure it's murder, then?" Thomas was positive it was, too, but he was curious about Larry's take on it.

"What else could it be, Thomas? My God, poisons don't get into stage props like that by accident!"

Thomas put up a restraining hand. "Larry, calm down. I'm just asking if it could have been, well," and he paused uncomfortably. "Could it have been suicide? It's not that I think it is, but the police will want to consider every possibility."

Larry was shaking his head, negating even the chance of such a thing. "Thomas, Eddie had so much going for him! His parents were well-off, he made excellent grades in school, Esther adored him and he was even accepted at Harvard, to start there next school year!" Larry looked up at Thomas, eyes reddened with sleeplessness. "He had no reason I can think of to do such a thing."

Thomas nodded. "You're probably right, Larry, and I understand what you're saying. I'm sorry I brought it up."

"Well, I shouldn't have reacted like I did. I just didn't get enough sleep last night, and I'm not sure how well I'll sleep tonight. But Sharon will be there tonight, and she can offer more consolation to Esther. I won't feel so helpless, to be truthful, and no doubt I'll sleep better." Larry looked at his watch. "I really need to get back to the pharmacy, Thomas. Thanks for having lunch with me, and filling me in about the other stuff. I'll tell Esther I got to see Eddie's license..." he frowned and shook his head. "Or should I? It will make her very curious to know why he was over there, and I won't know what to tell her!" He sighed as he stood up. "I'll have to think about that one!"

After walking back to the pharmacy with Larry, Thomas drove to the police station. This time, Detective Lamonde was there, and Thomas was shown in promptly.

Eric looked harried, his tie pulled open and his shirt rumpled. There were four or five half-smoked cigarettes stubbed out in his ashtray.

"Eric, you look terrible!" Thomas said.

"Well, thanks a lot! You don't look all that handsome, yourself," Eric retorted.

Thomas laughed. "I guess I deserved that. Are the burglaries getting you down, or is it something else?"

"We have a couple of strong leads on the burglaries, and there are a couple of the sergeants out doing the legwork right now." He sat down in his terminally squeaky chair, and gestured for Thomas to have a seat, too.

"We're a small town, so we have a small detective force," he began. "That means when cases come up, we all have to pitch in. Especially when it's a suspected homicide! Right now, I'm dealing with this death at Temple Beth Shalom."

Thomas nodded. "I was there when it happened, Eric, and I may have some information that will help."

Eric leaned forward in his chair. "You do? What sort of information? Did you overhear something at the play that night?"

Thomas held up a hand. "Wait, Eric. Let me go back a little bit. This starts with the strange figure who has been out in the pasture with the deer."

Eric snorted his disgust. "That? What does it have to do with the death of this Kusack boy?"

"The Kusack boy *was* the strange figure," Thomas said slowly. "And, just a couple of days ago, someone tried to shoot him while he was out in the field."

Eric looked amazed and skeptical. "OK, Thomas. You're going to have to convince me on this one." He crossed his arms, and leaned back in his chair, a bulldog frown on his face.

So, Thomas related all the events of the past week or so, going back to tie in with things he had already told Eric about the deer, the strange dancing figure, and so on. He told Eric how Eddie was a vegetarian, and a very strong anti-hunter, how he had been confronted by someone and almost gotten into a fight while passing out anti-hunting flyers before Halloween. And, he told him about Eddie's affinity with the squirrels in the park, how they had gone to Eddie when they wouldn't approach his girlfriend, Esther. Eric sat listening very patiently through all this, though his face registered skepticism.

Finally, he told about tracking the figure through the woods, and finding the driver's license near where someone parked a car on the side of the road. He took the license from his pocket and handed it to Eric.

"I would have brought it by much earlier, but it only became possible evidence in a murder case last night, Eric. I was going to try to return it to the owner," Thomas apologized. "I didn't even know until last night that Eddie Kusack was in the play, when Larry Meyer's daughter came down from the stage and said his name."

Eric was sitting and staring at the driver's license, eyes unfocused. Thomas stopped speaking, and the room was relatively silent for a few moments.

Eric looked up. "You know, that's one of the problems with living in a small town. People are just unwilling to believe that murderers can exist in their quiet little village. So, when something occurs like this shooting at someone in the pasture, the supposition is always that it's an accident, or that someone thought he was a deer." He dropped the license on his desk.

"I'll pull the reports that were filed by the investigating officers. It's significant that only uniformed cops came out that time to investigate. If they thought it really was an attempted shooting of a human being, they would have sent out a plainclothes detective to investigate."

"You have to admit, it does sound odd, even in retrospect: someone is in a field, petting wild deer. Someone fires at him, or them, and the deer scatter, then the unseen gunman fires at the fleeing figure," Thomas said.

"Yes, it does," Eric admitted, "but the possibility of an attempted shooting at a human should occur to a police officer, even if not to the everyday civilian. I did twelve years as a beat cop and detective in metro Atlanta, and killings are not always performed by 'lowlifes'. Sometimes they are done by average, run-of-the-mill people who are desperate, scared, angry or nervous. We don't like to think that way."

"Eric, do they know yet what killed Eddie?" Thomas asked.

"The complete results are not in, but the preliminary verdict is that it was some sort of caustic poison. The victim's throat and the inside of his mouth were red, swollen and inflamed."

"Like cyanide?"

Eric looked at Thomas with surprise. "Well, yes – cyanide could have been the poison. The female paramedic who was on the scene said she smelled bitter almonds when she tried to work on the victim." He snorted. "This thing about always being able to smell almonds when someone is poisoned with cyanide, that's a load of bunk. First of all, unless there is a lot of the cyanide, the smell may not be that strong. Secondly, only about six out of ten people have the ability to smell the scent of cyanide. It's a genetic thing, and most of the people who can, are women."

Eric looked curiously at Thomas. "What made you think of cyanide, anyway? Is it because, in the play, the character played by the victim dies of cyanide poisoning?"

"No, although now that you mention it, that is pretty odd! I was discussing Eddie's death with Larry Meyer, Esther Meyer's father, and he was describing what cyanide can do, and how a death from cyanide would look."

"How would Mr. Meyer know such a thing?" Eric squinted at Thomas as he asked.

"He owns Meyer's Pharmacy, downtown," Thomas explained.

"Ah, I see. Well, the final autopsy report will be available tomorrow morning, or maybe later today. The first ones we have to officially notify, of course, will be the parents," Eric said.

Thomas nodded, and said in a very quiet voice, "Especially since we have little Deanna in our family, I can't imagine such a thing happening. It's enough to give a parent nightmares."

"My son lives with my ex-wife, in North Carolina. He's twelve. I can't imagine what I would do if I got a call from someone saying he died from being poisoned while performing in a school play. I don't know how I'd handle it," Eric said in a low voice, looking down at his hands. "It's bad enough I don't get to see him very often."

"I didn't know, Eric," said Thomas. "I'm sorry."

Eric shrugged. "It's not something I talk about very much."

"Well, your relationship with your son just became a special part of my prayer list, nonetheless," Thomas assured him.

"Thanks, Thomas." Eric stood up. "Look, I really have a lot to do, and I have a meeting this afternoon with the rabbi of Beth Shalom, the principal of the school, and Eddie Kusack's teachers."

On the way home, Thomas stopped by the church building site. Things were definitely coming along. Some of the curbing had been laid around the edge of the parking area, although there was still only gravel to park on.

Thomas went inside and found Simon relaxing in a corner, watching some electricians running wires and cables across the ceiling, while carpenters installed insulation in the walls.

"Afternoon, pastor! How are you today?" Simon asked. But before Thomas could answer, Simon dropped the front legs of his chair down to the floor and stood up. "Let's go outside and get some fresh air," he suggested.

They went outside and leaned against Simon's pickup. "Well, what have you found out? I know you didn't bring me out here to enjoy the sunshine!" Thomas gestured up at the gray billows of clouds that only recently stopped dropping rain.

Simon grinned at him. "You're right, pastor! As you mighta noticed, that there Lance Hoskins is back at work today." Simon pointed out across the parking lot, toward a beat-up red pickup truck.

"He actually came in late Wednesday afternoon; got in a couple of hours work and left about 5:30. He wasn't real talkative Wednesday. And yesterday the boy was a real bundle of nerves! But this morning he's relaxed, joking, about as normal as I've seen him." But Simon was grinning like he had more to tell, so Thomas motioned for him to continue.

"Well, Lance got to bragging this morning about how he was going to be able to shoot at least one or two big deer, real soon. Some of the boys was razzin' him about why he hadn't already shot one, and he said somebody messed up his shots. But now, he says, that ain't gonna happen no more!" Simon peered intently at Thomas. "Does that mean anything to you, pastor? Hey, you OK?"

Simon's eyes were open wide now, and Thomas realized that he must have looked stunned, because that was certainly how he felt!

"I... I'm OK, Simon. Tell me, did Lance say why he'd be able to shoot deer now?"

Simon scratched the stubble on his jaw. "Funny thing, that. When someone asked him what happened, he said, 'the feller who's been stoppin' me has drunk himself to death.'"

Chapter 7

For, lo, the wicked bend their bow, they make ready their arrow upon the string, that they may privily shoot at the upright in heart.
Psalms 11:2

Thomas was nauseous with the feelings of anger and disgust he was experiencing. He turned away from Simon, who put his hand on Thomas's shoulder. "Pastor! Hey, are you gonna be OK?" There was genuine concern in the older man's voice.

Thomas nodded, as he put his head down. The nausea went away as quickly as it had come. It was the casual treatment of Eddie's death that brought it on.

"Yes, I'll be OK, Simon. It's just that I know someone who sort of 'drank himself to death', and it's the person who has been stopping the poachers from spotlighting the deer in the pasture across the road from the church!" Thomas stood up straighter and shook his head to clear the fog and anger from it. Simon looked shocked as he clutched at Thomas's arm.

"Who was it, pastor?" Simon asked.

"Eddie Kusack, a student over at Beth Shalom high school," said Thomas, and he proceeded to tell Simon most of what happened in the last couple of days since they spoke together.

"So," he finished, "Eddie did 'drink himself to death', by taking poison of some kind. Somehow, Lance knew about Eddie's death, and how it happened." Thomas stopped, thoughts racing through his mind. Was Lance the one who poisoned Eddie? If so, how did he do it?

"Pastor?" Simon's voice broke in on his thoughts. "Pastor? Do you think this feller Lance poisoned Eddie Kusack?"

"Simon, I only know that he somehow knew about it this morning, and the official news hasn't been released yet. But I don't know how he could have done it, since he doesn't even go to any high school any more, much less go to Beth Shalom High School."

Thomas looked down at his watch. "It's getting late, Simon, and I want to tell Detective Lamonde what you just told me. Is it OK with you that I mention your name?"

Simon chuckled. "No problem, pastor. You know, I went out there to visit Eric and his wife once last month, to help 'em with plantin' some fall flowers and a few vegetables in a plot in their back yard. He's learnin'."

They shook hands and he left while Simon went back into the church. As Thomas drove away, he looked at his watch again, and realized that he'd probably need to call Eric on his cell phone if he wanted to catch him before he left the office.

"Detective Lieutenant Lamonde – may I help you?"

"Eric, this is Thomas. I have some information you might want."

"Boy, you barely caught me. I have my raincoat in my hand, and my hat on my head." Thomas heard him sit down in the squeaky chair. "What is it?"

"You know Simon Daniels, right?"

Eric laughed. "Sure do! He's been over here to help us with our back yard garden. And it's been doing better this year, too!"

"Well, he is acting as a sort of unofficial 'supervisor' over at the new church site. The person who owns that truck that I was suspicious about – remember it? Well, he works there as an electrician."

"Really? Has anything odd happened over there?" Eric sounded only moderately interested.

"Because I was suspicious, I asked Simon to keep an eye and ear open for anything unusual, especially anyone bragging about spotlighting deer or anything like that." Thomas gasped as he almost hit a car, so he pulled over into a gas station parking lot to continue the conversation.

"And did he hear anything?" Eric asked.

"Not until this morning. The driver of that truck, Lance Hoskins, was bragging about how he was going to get his limit of deer very soon. The others were giving him a hard time about not getting one yet.

"He came back with the idea that someone else spoiled all his shots, but that it wasn't going to happen any more."

Thomas heard a quick intake of breath on the other end. "Thomas, did he say why?"

"I was coming to that. He said, 'the fellow who's been stopping me has drunk himself to death.'"

"Simon actually heard him say that?" Eric asked in an excited voice.

"Yes, he did. He was standing a few feet away, pretending to do something else." Thomas waited a few seconds, then asked, "Eric? Are you there?"

"Yeah, yeah – I'm here. I'm just trying to figure out how to use this. Did this Hoskins say just when he was going to shoot a deer?"

"No, but this is the weekend, and that makes it easier. I figure it will be tonight or tomorrow night."

"Hmmm. We could have some people staking out the area around the field, or maybe the roads near there. If they could be out of sight, someone parked behind the church would hear the gunshot and then we could box him in, maybe." Thomas could almost hear the gears turning in Eric's head as he tried to come up with a way. "I need to go, Thomas. If we are going to try to do this tonight, I have to get it organized in a hurry. And thanks! Oh, by the way, do you have any problem with us having a man parked behind the church?"

"Not a problem at all. Just catch these guys. Even if they aren't the ones who killed Eddie, they knew about it, and how he died, before the news was released. Maybe they can help you catch whoever DID do it."

Thomas got home in time to stop Amy from being upset about cold supper. After giving thanks for the meal, he loaded up his plate and proceeded to tell Amy about all the things he learned that day. Of course, that almost made supper completely cold, because they were so engrossed in the topic they barely took time to eat.

At a little after 7:00 PM, the phone rang. It was Detective Lamonde.

"Thomas, I wanted let you know we will have a man parked behind your church. I've gotten the authorization for three cars – one behind your church, and two unmarked vehicles parked on side roads near you."

Thomas looked out the window as he was on the phone. "What time should the car behind the church be arriving?"

"Should any time now. We don't want to get started so late that the perps see us getting into place."

"Yes, that's why I was asking. It's getting pretty dark out there already." Thomas saw lights approaching on the road, and a black-and-white slowed, then pulled into the church parking lot. "Eric, I think he just arrived."

"Good. I'll be in contact with them by radio until around midnight, and they'll contact me if anything happens after then." Eric sounded confident and a little excited.

"I'll probably know about anything happening before you do, Eric, but I'll want to know all the details as soon as you can give them to me."

Eric chuckled. "Don't worry, Thomas. After helping us to set up this little trap, you deserve to know the details as soon as it's legal to give them to you."

"Remember, I didn't guarantee that anything would happen at all, much less tonight." Thomas cautioned.

"Hey, I know that. That's the way a stakeout is – it's like going fishing. Sometimes you catch the fish, sometimes they aren't there, and sometimes they get away."

There was a policewoman ringing the doorbell, so Thomas got off the phone with Eric. He conferred with her for a few minutes, and she left to park her car behind the church.

Amy came into the kitchen in response to the doorbell. "Thomas, who was that?"

"It was the police. They're going to do a stakeout tonight to try to catch the poachers. They want to question that guy Hoskins that I told you about." He sat down with Amy at the kitchen table after pouring them each a cup of coffee. "There will be unmarked cars parked on little side roads east and west of here, and a patrol car parked behind the church. When she hears the gunshot, she'll radio the others. They will come out onto the main road and box in the poachers' vehicle."

"Which we hope will be that Hoskins guy, right?" Amy asked.

"Exactly."

79

Thomas and Amy spent the rest of the evening trying to ignore the tension created by the presence of police cars hiding around the church. They watched television for a little while, then Thomas sat down and read the Bible while Amy worked on a presentation for the Ladies' Auxiliary meeting the following week.

About 10:30 there was a loud report outside, and Thomas rushed to the window, but it was only an old car backfiring as it slowed down. Thomas looked out and saw that there were two deer in the field, probably what the driver of the car slowed down to see.

In spite of the anxiety of waiting, Amy and Thomas managed to convince themselves to try to get some sleep at about 11:30. Deanna had already given up and was comfortably tucked into her baby bed. She had no notion of the stresses her parents were experiencing.

Although Thomas doubted he would be able to sleep, he must have, because he was awakened once more by gunshots reverberating outside. He jerked bolt upright and looked at the glowing face of the alarm clock by the bed. It read: 2:50 AM.

Rolling out of bed, Thomas grabbed his robe, avoiding turning on any lights to alert the poachers that they were being noticed. This time there was no gunning of the engine or squealing tires following the gunshots.

When Thomas focused the night vision scope out the front window, he was unsurprised to see a beat-up pickup truck. He couldn't tell the color because of the overall green look of anything seen through the night vision, but he was sure it was the same one. Scanning the area, he saw that one person was out of the truck and in the field, looking at what appeared to be a deer carcass. There were two others in the pickup truck.

He wanted to try to see the license plate, so he pushed the switch to make the infrared illumination come on.

There! He could see the license plate clearly now. But within seconds he saw the two in the cab of the truck start turning around and looking, as if searching for something. Then one of them reached over and blew the horn on the truck, waving frantically at the person in the pasture.

That person turned and, after hesitating, dropped the deer he was dragging and ran toward the truck. He clambered over the barbed-wire fence, becoming stuck there. Bright lights suddenly shone on both the truck and the fence-climber, and the sound of a siren combined with flashing blue lights bouncing across the landscape to let Thomas know the police car had rolled out from behind the church.

Thomas put down the night vision scope and watched the drama unfold. The police cruiser pulled across the road, blocking the pickup from proceeding any further east. One of the passengers in the truck slid over under the wheel and immediately tried to back up and turn around. In their haste and panic, the driver backed the pickup truck into a deep ditch, where the back wheels spun without gaining purchase.

Moments after that, unmarked cars with flashing blue lights in their grills sped to a stop, one of them blocking the road on the other side of the pickup.

Officers were out of the cars now, announcing through bullhorns that they were arresting the person at the fence, as well as those in the cab of the pickup. Two of the police officers disentangled the one poacher from the fence, while the others were herded by the policewoman who had been parked behind the church for the last few hours, her pistol at the ready.

A hand lightly touched Thomas's shoulder, and he flinched. "Don't worry, it's just me," said his wife. "The sirens woke me up, combined with the blue strobes flashing through the windows." She stood beside Thomas, her other hand clutching her robe closed around her. "They caught them!"

Each of the three prisoners was transported in a separate police vehicle; Thomas presumed this was to keep them from coordinating their stories. Soon a tow truck arrived and took the pickup truck away to the impound lot.

Thomas turned around and Amy hugged him. "There, honey! Now you should be able to sleep better. You tossed for so long before you finally settled down to sleep earlier." She kissed him, and he smiled.

"Yes, the big tension for the night is over. Now it just comes down to what happens at the police station. I'll have to rely on Eric for that information, though," Thomas said with a yawn.

* * *

The next day Thomas restrained himself from trying to call Eric. Plus, the youth group had a late afternoon activity that he needed to attend. By 8:00 PM, though, the barbecue grills were put away and the volleyball nets rolled up, so he could go back to the parsonage and call Eric.

There was no answer at his office, so Thomas took the initiative and called Eric at home.

"Lamonde residence," said a female voice.

"Maria, this is Thomas Wilson. How have you been?"

"Thomas! Very well, thanks. But I'll bet you didn't call here to ask me that. I'll get Eric for you." He heard the phone being placed on a hard surface, then muffled voices in the background.

"Thomas, how are you?" Eric said over the phone.

"I'm fine, but very curious about what may have resulted from last night's stakeout!"

There was a heavy sigh from the other end of the phone. "Thomas, we got some information, but not what we wanted. Hoskins is still in jail. The other two were released on bond."

"Can you tell me what you found out?" Thomas asked.

"Hoskins admitted that he had been trying to poach at that field. And he admitted that he had been frustrated by someone who was messing up his shots by scaring the deer. But he denied shooting specifically at Eddie Kusack, and he denied poisoning him. He has an alibi for the night Kusack was shot at – he was at a movie with his girlfriend, and was seen by others, besides having the ticket stubs."

"What about Thursday night? Did he have an alibi for that night?"

"No, he didn't. But we also don't have a witness that can place him at the scene, so we don't have a lot to go on there," Eric stated. "Unless someone can say he was there, or we find his fingerprints, we can't do a lot about that."

"But how did he know about Eddie's death, and how it happened? That remark about 'drunk himself to death' was very close to the mark!" Thomas was indignant. "And did the coroner determine what it was that killed Eddie?"

"He says he heard about it as gossip at work, that he doesn't remember who said it," replied Eric. "And the death was poisoning caused by sodium cyanide."

"Larry was right then. And do you really believe Hoskins about where he found out about it?"

"Thomas, you and I know he is lying, but we can't prove it and we can't get the truth from him if he won't give it to us," Eric reminded him.

"Then why is Hoskins still in jail?" Thomas wondered.

83

"Oh, that!" Eric laughed. "We got statements from the other two that verified Hoskins was the one who shot at your house that night. That's a felony, so he's being held for reckless endangerment, in addition to the charges for poaching, discharging a firearm from a vehicle and discharging a firearm from a public highway."

"Oh. Well, that was a very dangerous thing for him to do, and I'm glad he is in jail for that, at least," Thomas said. "Who were the other two?"

"A juvenile, and an older kid named Brian Benson."

Chapter 8

He sitteth in the lurking places of the villages: in the secret places doth he murder the innocent: his eyes are privily set against the poor. He lieth in wait secretly as a lion in his den: he lieth in wait to catch the poor: he doth catch the poor, when he draweth him into his net.
Psalms 4:8,9

For a moment Thomas froze. Why did he know that name? Then he gasped.

"Eric, did you say Brian Benson? Dark hair, about 19 years old?" he asked, breathless.

"Yes, that sounds like him. Why?" Eric was interested now. "Do you know something about him that I don't?"

"Well, if it's the same boy, he is Esther Meyer's ex-boyfriend. I met him at the play the other night, after Eddie collapsed on stage and everything was in an uproar."

"So, he was at the play. But what made you react that way?"

"Eric, when Esther came out from backstage, she was distraught. She went to her father, Larry, and collapsed in his arms, crying."

"That's understandable. Eddie was her boyfriend, and she'd just seen him die," Eric said.

"Yes, but in a few moments this kid Brian came up and tried to get her to talk to him, ostensibly to offer her comfort. She became very upset at him, and he was insistent about talking to her. I had to threaten him with taking him to the police that were on the premises, for making a scene, just to get him to leave them alone.

"Later, Larry told me that he was her ex-boyfriend, and was trying to persuade Esther to get back together with him," Thomas said.

"Hmmm. So you think this Benson kid may have had a motive to kill Eddie? Just because he moved in on his ex-girlfriend?" Eric sounded dubious.

"Eric, you didn't see his reaction. When I told him that he shouldn't be bothering Larry and Esther right then, he became very hostile toward me. It was only the threat of getting the police involved that made him leave them alone, I think. He was none too happy with me, I can tell you that!"

Eric said thoughtfully, "And since he was there, he could very well have had access to the fake whiskey. And he could have been the one who told Hoskins about Eddie Kusack's death from the poison."

"Exactly what I was thinking."

"But how would this kid have access to sodium cyanide?"

"That, I don't know. Maybe someone else got it for him."

"Thomas, this is getting more and more twisted. But listen," and his voice became very official and stern, "I don't want you to get involved and put yourself in danger like you did before!"

"Eric, I didn't go up there to the Henderson's to put myself in danger. I went up there to warn my friend and church member, Betty Henderson. It's not my fault that those criminals were there," Thomas protested.

Eric's reply was a mumbled growling sound, followed by an "OK, well, be more careful!"

* * *

Thomas and Amy had the first uneventful night, unmarked by possible gunshots and police activity, that they had experienced in weeks. Strangely enough, he had a hard time falling asleep. After lying beside a sleeping Amy for over an hour, he got up and went into the living room to sit, read the Bible, think and pray.

After reading four or five chapters in First Corinthians, Thomas closed his Bible, turned off the lamp beside his chair and sat in the darkness with just the Lord and his thoughts.

Lord, Thomas prayed, *what is happening here? We fought a battle with Satan over trying to build a new church, and by your grace and assistance the police were able to stop those trying to hinder us. Here is a new threat coming against us, but in a less direct fashion. Evil is attacking someone else, making the church a bystander – are we supposed to let this go because the people who are being harmed are not part of the body of Christ? I have a hard time with that, Lord.*

Thomas sat quietly for a while, waiting for that "still small voice" that Elijah heard. He heard nothing audible. With a sigh, he turned on the light, then picked up his Bible again and opened it. It fell open to Proverbs, and a beam of light from the lamp shone directly upon chapter 11, verse 11. He read, his lips moving silently: "If thou forbear to deliver them that are drawn unto death, and those that are ready to be slain; If thou sayest, Behold, we knew it not; doth not he that pondereth the heart consider it? and he that keepeth thy soul, doth not he know it? and shall not he render to every man according to his works?" He read the verses through again, and sat quietly considering this answer to his question.

If Christians would not intervene when they knew others were in trouble, if they turned their back and said, "Hey, it's not my concern," wouldn't God know it? Wouldn't God see their lack of action? Thomas smiled. It wasn't an audible voice, but it was as direct an answer as he could ask for, certainly. He couldn't be foolish about it – God neither expects nor wants that, he reasoned. But he couldn't ignore it, either.

Those thoughts gave Thomas some peace, so he went back to bed, pulled the covers up over himself and turned out the light.

* * *

The next day, the church was packed again, a condition that both delighted and concerned Thomas. He was glad to see people there, but hoped that the lack of seating (a temporary condition, since the new church was about half finished) didn't put anyone off from coming back.

At the end of the service he invited Simon Daniels to stand and give a quick progress report on the new church. Simon stood and let everyone know how the church was coming along, as well as making encouraging remarks about the roominess of the new building.

There was a brief spatter of applause, and Simon blushed as he nodded to everyone before sitting down again. The closing benediction was given, and several people went to talk to Simon about the new church, its facilities and how soon he thought it would be ready. Thomas smiled. This was just what Simon needed – to be drawn into more of the circles of fellowship within the church.

After most of the attendees had left the church, Simon came by to shake Thomas's hand and speak with him. "So, what happened with the poachers? Anything else come to light?"

Thomas grinned as he regarded Simon. "Simon, I get the distinct impression that this 'detective' work is something you enjoy."

Simon grinned back at Thomas. "Well, I was a retired farmer until just a few months ago. Then I got involved with this new church buildin', and my life got all excitin' again. Can't say it don't worry me some, but I can't say it's borin', either."

"Just so you know, Simon, they caught the Hoskins boy early Saturday morning, trying to poach another deer," Thomas told him. "There were two other boys in the truck with him. One of them was a juvenile, so that name hasn't been released to the public yet. The other was a young man named Brian Benson. Lance Hoskins is still in jail, but the other two have been released on bond."

Simon nodded, a satisfied smile on his face. "Glad to hear he's still in jail, anyway, pastor! But do they know if he was involved in the murder of that other boy?"

"They haven't finished their investigation, Simon. And until they do, please keep the details of this to yourself. We don't want to mess up the investigation by tipping anyone off that they might be under suspicion."

"I understand, pastor. Appreciate you tellin' me all you did!" He shook Thomas's hand and left.

Thomas started home for the parsonage, and looked over across the road at the pasture. To his amazement, there were three deer grazing in the field - in the middle of the day! They seemed oblivious to the fact that the sun was high in the sky, or that cars were zooming by less than thirty yards away. Thomas stood and watched the deer for some time, puzzled by this atypical behavior.

Just as a test, he walked closer to the road. The deer did not seem to notice or care. He picked up a rock from the side of the road, drew back, and hurled it with all his might. It landed about 20 feet from the nearest deer. The deer simply looked up for a moment, then went back to grazing. Frowning, Thomas put both his hands to his mouth as a funnel, and shouted, "HEY!" at the deer. They all three raised their heads, and one took a step or two, but within a minute or so they resumed grazing once more.

Thomas ambled thoughtfully to the parsonage then, pondering the strange docility of these wild animals. Deer did grow accustomed to human contact, he knew, but he had never seen deer outside of a park or zoo that were so placid and calm.

After lunch, while Deanna was napping and Amy was reading, Thomas decided to call Stan Bowman.

"Hello, pastor! Is there something I can do for you?" he asked.

"Stan, you've had more experience with hunting deer than I have. I've only shot a couple in my whole life. I've got a question about how they act."

"Sure, pastor. What sort of questions do you have?"

"You know about the deer that have been showing up in the pasture across from the church, because we have been talking about it lately."

"Right, I remember that."

"Don't deer usually feed in early morning, late afternoon or in the middle of the night? Especially when it's hunting season, and they feel threatened by all the hunters in the woods?"

"That's pretty accurate, pastor. Of course, now and then you'll see a foolish young deer out in the middle of the day, but even then they are pretty skittish! They high-tail it if you come close to them," Stan replied.

"That's what I thought! Stan, there were three deer out in that pasture when I left the church today, at a little before 1:00 PM."

Stan sounded a little puzzled, but more amused. "Well, I guess they haven't learned yet, have they?"

"But that's not all. I went closer to them, and it didn't bother them. I threw a rock that landed within about 20 feet of them, and one of them just lifted his head and went back to eating. Finally, I shouted at them as loud as I could, and all they did was raise their heads for a little while, then they went back to grazing!" Thomas was emphatic. "I've never seen any wild deer so immune to being disturbed."

Stan Bowman sounded very puzzled now. "I have to admit that certainly is strange! I can understand them being out in the middle of the day, perhaps if they were very hungry. But to not be disturbed by a thrown rock, and by a loud yell, is downright weird! Did they look sick or anything?"

"No, they appeared to be fat and happy. Just grazing away, without a single concern in the world," Thomas stated.

"I've never heard of a wild deer acting like that. Now, a tame deer, or one in a park or something like that, they get used to humans being around and it doesn't bother them as much. But even those deer will interpret a loud, sudden noise as something frightening, maybe a noise made by a predator, and they'll run. It's just in their nature." Stan chuckled. "Now, I have heard of a single deer ignoring being shot at, just standing there and waiting for the hunter to take a second shot. But I've never been that lucky, and I doubt that a group of three deer would do that. If even one alerted and ran, all of them would."

"Thanks, Stan, I thought that was the case, but I wanted to confirm it with someone with more deer experience than I have. I wonder what could cause them to act like that," he mused.

"Honestly, I really don't know, unless they had somehow been tranquilized!" Stan laughed. "I don't know anyone who goes around treating deer for bad nerves, though."

Thomas laughed, too, and they hung up. He stood there by the phone, tapping on it with his fingertips as he mused on the strange behavior of the deer. If they were THAT calm, maybe it wasn't so amazing that Eddie Kusack got so close to them, even touching them if they knew his scent. But what was making them that way?

* * *

After the service that night, another peaceful night passed at the parsonage, with nothing to disturb Thomas and Amy's sleep. But Eddie Kusack's funeral was Monday, and Thomas was going to attend. Although he didn't know Eddie personally, he felt an odd sort of connection because of all that had happened with the pasture and the deer. And of course, the Meyer family were good friends to Amy and himself, and he wanted to be supportive.

So, at 10:00 AM, Thomas was sitting in Temple Beth Shalom, with a paper yarmulka on his head, given to him by one of the ushers. Beside him sat Larry Meyer, Sharon Meyer and a red-eyed Esther. The chanting of the Kiddush rang sonorously throughout the synagogue.

After the service, Larry and Thomas took a few minutes to talk in an out-of-the-way corner.

"Thomas, thanks so much for coming. It meant a lot to Esther to see you here. She said so to me," Larry said, grasping Thomas's hand.

"Esther is a great young lady, and I very much feel for her loss. Tell me – am I correct that the couple sitting at the center of the front right-hand pew were Eddie's parents? It must have been so hard for them to hear such a thing and rush back from their trip like that!"

Larry nodded. "Oh, yes. It was terrible. Eddie's mother almost collapsed twice at the funeral home this weekend. That's not to say his father wasn't hurting too, but Sam is a very strong personality. Plus, I believe he felt a responsibility to Jeannette to be strong for her, you know?"

"Have you heard anything more about the investigation, Larry?"

"No, not really. I hear rumors, you know – nothing more."

Thomas looked around to be sure they were not being overheard. "Did you hear about the confirmation of the poison?"

Larry's eyes grew wider as he, too, looked about them. "No. What was it?"

"Larry, please – please don't share this with anyone yet, but I felt an obligation to tell you. You guessed right. It was cyanide – sodium cyanide, specifically."

Larry's face twisted into a look of pain. "And none of us realized he wasn't acting when he grabbed his throat and collapsed. My God!" He shut his eyes, and bowed his head.

Thomas put his hand on Larry's shoulder. "Larry, listen! You couldn't know, none of us could – except for the poisoner."

Larry looked up at Thomas, anger in his face. "You know something else that's sad? As much as I liked Eddie, I'd really like to catch the person who did this because of the impact it had on Esther! She is miserable."

"I'm glad Sharon is back now," Thomas said. "That should help things, anyway."

Larry nodded. "Yeah, they have a very good relationship, and Esther has been leaning on her mother a lot."

Thomas considered for a moment, then said quietly, "Larry, I have some questions I'd like to ask Esther, if you don't mind. They're about Eddie. I don't want to do anything that would upset her, but it might help her to talk, and it might help me to figure out a couple of things that have been bothering me, too."

"The detective that came out and spoke with Esther didn't seem to connect with her very well," Larry admitted. "There was some sort of friction between the two of them, even though the detective was female. I don't know what it was." He looked at Thomas. "Esther has always respected you and Amy. I don't see what it could hurt. I know you wouldn't ask anything that would intentionally cause pain for her."

Thomas smiled. "Thanks, Larry. When do you think would be good to come over?"

"How about tomorrow night, say 7:00 PM? Would that be OK?" Larry asked.

"Sure, no problem," Thomas replied, and they walked out of the synagogue. Thomas embraced both Sharon and Esther, and then left for home.

When Thomas arrived at home, Amy was at a meeting of the Ladies Auxiliary, but there was a note on the kitchen table telling him to call Eric Lamonde. He rang up the police station and asked for Detective Lamonde.

"Eric, this is Thomas. Did you want something?"

"Thomas, thanks for calling me back. Remember that policeman who came out and collected the spent rifle shell that day?"

"Yes, I remember. He and I got pretty wet, walking through the field."

"Well, it was a .30-06 cartridge casing that he found."

"Yes, I remember that, too. We both sniffed the casing, and it seemed to have been very recently fired."

"Yeah. Unfortunately, we struck out on two different areas. First of all, the rifle that the Hoskins boy used to poach the deer, or try to poach them, is a .30-30 caliber, not .30-06. Secondly, the mud and water had obliterated all but bare traces of fingerprints from the casing, and there are none that are usable for identification." Eric sounded very disappointed.

"And I guess Hoskins doesn't have access to a rifle in the other caliber. But that doesn't affect your case against him for the poaching and all the other charges, does it? It just disqualifies him as the person who shot at Eddie that night, right?" Thomas asked.

"True, but I was hoping to tie up all the loose ends quickly on this. It just isn't working out that way." Eric cleared his throat. "So... I just wanted to know if there was anything else you may have remembered about that night, or about the night at the play, that might help us in any way."

"Eric, I can't think of anything right now, but I will be sure to let you know of any details that come to mind. Believe me, I want to catch this person, too!" Thomas paused, then continued. "I am supposed to go over to Larry Meyers's house tomorrow night and visit with them. I'm going to spend some time talking with Esther, and maybe something will come from that conversation.

"But there is something odd I have noticed in the last couple of days. Remember when I told you about the person I saw who appeared to be petting the deer?" Thomas asked.

"Yeah, that was Eddie Kusack."

"Right. Well, Larry told me that Esther related to him that Eddie seemed to have a very good relationship with animals in general – squirrels in the park, that sort of thing." He heard Eric snort on the other end of the phone, but continued. "But we both know that wild deer are not as easily approached as squirrels in a park, which have been conditioned to the presence of humans."

"Yeah, I know that. That's why I was, well, let's say doubtful about the details of your statement," Eric said.

"That's a polite way to say it! But I understand. The thing is, yesterday I saw something very weird. There were deer in the pasture in the middle of the day, about 1:00. Now, that's odd enough by itself, as it was a clear, sunny day, and most deer are spooked this time of year because of the hunters wandering through the woods.

"Well, these deer seemed to be very docile, almost tranquilized. I tossed a rock close to them, and even yelled at them at the top of my lungs, with no more reaction from them than raising their heads and looking around," Thomas finished and waited for a reaction from Eric.

"Hmmm. I dunno, Thomas. What does a herd of deer that are not shy of humans have to do with this case?" Eric sounded intrigued but puzzled.

Frustrated, Thomas answered, "I'm not really sure, Eric. But it's just so strange, I thought I should tell you about it."

Thomas heard Eric sigh. "I'll keep it in mind, Thomas. This case is sort of weird, anyway, so you never know what might become a lead, eventually. But you'll let me know if anything turns up from your conversation with the Meyers's, right?"

"Sure, Eric. No problem."

Amy arrived home from the meeting, with Deanna snoozing in her baby carrier. Thomas met her at the door, taking Deanna from her and giving each of them a kiss.

Amy plopped herself down on the couch and slipped off her shoes. She looked up at Thomas and he could see she was upset.

"What's the matter, Amy? Meeting didn't go well?"

Amy pressed her lips together, then said with vehemence, "You know, Thomas, I love our church, and I love our members, but I get so frustrated sometimes by their attitudes I could just scream!"

Thomas's brow creased and he sat down beside her. "Honey, can you wait and scream later? You'll wake Deanna!" He squeezed her hand and grinned at her. She whipped her head around to look at him, then realized she was being teased, and smiled a little.

"Oh, alright – I won't scream right now. But, oohh, sometimes some of these people can be so, so..."

"Human?" Thomas asked.

"Yes! That's it – human. Isn't it supposed to be true that the new man overcomes the old nature when you become a Christian? I tell you, I got very frustrated today by someone in the group who was making snide remarks about Jews being killed, and how their past was catching up with them. It was all I could do to be polite, and remind everyone there that, after all, the Jews were God's chosen people, and that Jesus was Jewish, too." Amy's hazel eyes were hawklike with anger.

"Who was it?" Thomas wondered.

"Oh, it was Mrs. Martinson. She is one of those people that I sometimes wish would find another church to attend, you know?" Amy was shaking her head.

"Ah, yes – the Martinsons." Thomas nodded. He knew the whole family. Christians in name and profession, they were narrow-minded bigots who were convinced that anyone whose beliefs differed in the slightest from their own was wrong. He knew that several of his sermons had caused their eyebrows to go almost into their hairlines, but that didn't stop him from preaching what he believed and what the Bible said.

"Honey, I understand. It makes me angry, too, and I believe it's a righteous indignation. But maybe, if they continue to hear the truth of God's word preached, they will eventually come to understand and believe it. And there are their children to consider, too. At least here, we know they are getting exposed to wholesome Christianity, not some warped version that preaches hatred and bigotry."

She pulled in a deep breath. "Well, thanks for letting me get it off my chest, anyway. I just needed to vent." She tucked her feet up under herself as she sat on the sofa. "How did the funeral go?"

"It was a beautiful service, but very sad for everyone there. It's always so heartbreaking to lose a young person, and especially in such an unexpected and sudden manner," he said. "And Larry is even more upset than I expected him to be. He is angry, not only over Eddie's murder, but about the impact Eddie's death is having on Esther. It's really hit her hard, according to him."

"She was really torn apart the other night," Amy agreed. "I felt so sorry for her."

"Larry was glad you were there, since Sharon wasn't home yet. But she is home now – I saw her at the funeral service,"

Thomas said. "Oh, and I'm going there tomorrow night to see Esther and talk with her a little about Eddie."

Amy frowned. "Why, Thomas?"

Thomas paused, trying to think of a way to answer this question. Finally, choosing his words carefully, he said, "Amy, I know I'm not part of the police force. But this young man was shot at in the field across from our home, as I watched him. And then on the night we went to the play, he was murdered by some unknown assailant, using a poison, while we sat and watched. I don't know – somehow, I feel an obligation to help to discover who did this, and make sure they don't do it again."

"Thomas, you're not a detective! You're a minister of the gospel. The police have the responsibility of finding Eddie's murderer," Amy protested.

Thomas nodded. "And I agree with that, up to a point. But Amy, the detective they sent to interview Esther didn't seem to connect with her very well. Maybe she's a bigot like Mrs. Martinson, or maybe there was some other reason. But Esther has always respected both you and me, and I'm hoping she will tell me things that she couldn't open up about with the investigating officer." His eyes widened at a sudden thought. "Or maybe she'll tell you!"

Amy started to shake her head, then looked at Thomas's face. "Thomas, I'm not a detective, either. I don't know what to ask her."

"I know we aren't. But I have some things I would like to know about Eddie, and about his relationships with others in the school, that she can probably tell us. You have a better rapport with her than I do, honey. If I go over the basic questions with you, will you talk with her and see what she says? It's important, you know that."

Amy looked doubtful.

"Honey," he said, taking her hand, "I'm not asking you to trick her. I've been up front with Larry about this, and I'll be up front with Esther, too. But there are some things that, if we know them, could help the police figure out who killed Eddie."

Amy was shaking her head. "Oh, Thomas, I don't know..."

Chapter 9

The God of my rock; in him will I trust: he is my shield, and the horn of my salvation, my high tower, and my refuge, my saviour; thou savest me from violence.

2nd Samuel 22:3

The next morning Thomas called Larry at the pharmacy and asked if it was OK to bring Amy and Deanna along to visit, too.

"Of course, Thomas! I don't think Esther has seen Deanna at all, and Sharon only saw her right after the adoption," Larry was effusive. "The sight of a young, new life might be a good thing for Esther – let her know that life goes on, and that there are still beautiful things happening in the world."

"That's a good idea, Larry. Deanna's growing a lot, and her hair is really getting thick. We believe she's going to turn out to be a redhead," Thomas said.

"I'll call Sharon and let her know you all are coming. She'll want to know."

"Listen, Larry," Thomas protested, "we're not coming for a meal or anything like that. We don't want to cause any more trouble or stress for any of you. We just want to visit."

Larry put on his thickest Brooklyn Yiddish accent, "Oh-HO! So our food isn't good enough for you, Mr. High-and-Mighty Wilson? Well, I got news for you – my Sharon is not going to let ANYBODY leave her house without putting on at least a pound or two, eh?"

Thomas laughed in spite of himself. "Oh, OK, but not a meal. Just a snack or something. And we'll bring something, too, alright?"

"That's not necessary, but if you want to, you know you can," Larry replied. "We'll see you at 7:00, then. And no wine: I remember you two don't drink."

On the way to the Meyers's house, Thomas and Amy stopped and picked up a fruit tray at Wiggleston's. The Meyers lived in a two-story home on the outskirts of Pennington, in a modestly upscale neighborhood. Thomas carried Deanna in, with Amy following with the fruit tray.

Sharon was very demonstrative in her greetings, hugging both Amy and Thomas, and exclaiming over how much Deanna had grown. Before they even got into the living room, Sharon had Deanna out of her carrier, and was cuddling her close.

"Oh, Amy, she reminds me so much of Esther! It's so nice to hold a little baby, and remember those times," she said in a tender voice. "Right, Larry?" she directed at her husband, who had just walked into the room with Esther in tow.

"Absolutely, although I haven't gotten to hold Deanna yet, since you grabbed her up as soon as she got in the door!" Larry came over and tickled Deanna, who was looking around with wide eyes but seemed to be enjoying the attention.

"Hello, Esther," Amy said and gave the young lady a hug. Esther's eyes were still a little red, but it didn't look like she had been crying in the last couple of hours, anyway.

"Hi, Mrs. Wilson, and Reverend Wilson. Thanks for coming to the funeral, Reverend Wilson. It was very nice of you," she said.

"I'm sorry I couldn't be there," Amy said, "but I had a prior engagement that I couldn't get out of."

"That's alright, I understand." Esther sat down in a big, overstuffed chair and tucked her feet up under herself. Her mother took Deanna over and showed her to Esther.

"Isn't she a doll? I told Thomas and Amy she looks just like you when you were a baby!"

Esther smiled. "Yeah, I heard, Mom. Can I hold her?" she asked, looking over at Amy.

"Sure, Esther!"

Esther took Deanna from her mother, and laid the baby in her lap, so she could look down at Deanna and play with her. The adults exchanged glances, and Larry got up from the sofa.

"Well, anybody want something to drink? We've got coffee, hot tea, cocoa, and soda if you want it," he inquired.

Thomas gestured at the fruit tray Amy had placed on a sidetable. "We brought some fresh fruit – hope that's acceptable payment for your hospitality!"

Larry opened his mouth for a retort, when Sharon broke in. "Don't start, you two!" She looked at Amy. "Honestly, it's like they're a couple of 12-year-olds when they get together like this – always teasing each other!" She got up and took the fruit tray. "I'll put this in the kitchen, and get the drinks ready, while you two sit and talk."

Larry stepped over and took the tray from her hands. "No, honey, Thomas and I will take care of the drinks. You want decaf, right? Amy?"

"Decaf for me, too, Larry."

"Right. Come on, Thomas." He went through the swinging door into the kitchen, followed by Thomas. Larry placed the fruit on the kitchen counter, and started pulling out the necessary items to make coffee.

"You want decaf, too, Thomas?" he asked.

"Hot tea, if you have it, thanks."

"No problem. Hmm... let's see. We have chamomile, Irish breakfast, green tea, spice tea and rooibos." He turned and looked at Thomas. Thomas picked out his tea, and dropped the teabag into a mug.

Thomas looked over at the door, through which they could hear a faint murmur. "By the way, my compliments on how you managed to get us out of the way so the women could talk with Esther. Nicely done," he said in a low voice.

Larry grinned as he put decaf coffee into the drip coffeemaker. "Well, when you said you wanted to bring Amy over, I thought it might be more than just to be sociable. I saw how those two were interacting the other night after the play. Esther really connected with Amy." He switched on the coffeemaker.

The hot water was ready. Larry poured the hot water over the teabags in the two mugs., then leaned back against the countertop as the tea and coffee brewed, crossing his arms and regarding Thomas steadily. "So, are you going to tell me what you are trying to find out?"

"Some of it I don't know myself, Larry. Here is what I know, in a nutshell: I know that Eddie was a kid with strong ideas about humane treatment of both people and animals. And, I believe that is why he was showing up in the field across from the church and parsonage, to keep others from shooting those deer." Thomas frowned, then continued.

"But why that field, and those deer? There are literally thousands of places around Pennington where he could have been an anti-hunting rebel, yet he chose that field. Did Eddie live close to the church, so it was easy for him?" Thomas asked.

"No, he lived on the other side of Pennington, about eight miles away. It wouldn't be convenient at all," Larry replied.

"Well, there you go. Why that field and those deer?" Thomas stared at the steam rising from the steeping teabags. "You know, I wonder if it has anything to do with the strange deer in that field!"

Larry checked on the progress of the coffee, and turned his attention back to Thomas. "Strange? What's so strange about them?"

"They're... well, they're almost tame and docile. Remember, I told you how I saw Eddie, or someone, standing in the field with their hand resting on the back of a deer?" Larry nodded and Thomas continued, "I was leaving the church this past Sunday, at almost one o'clock in the afternoon. There was a bright sun, and quite a few cars were zooming by on the road.

"There were three deer grazing, less than thirty yards from the highway. They showed no nervousness whatsoever. They simply kept eating, no matter what sort of vehicle went by.

"Then I threw a stone at them, and it landed about twenty feet from the closest one, with very little effect. I even yelled as loud as I could, and the deer just raised their heads and looked around, then went back to eating! That's not normal deer behavior, Larry."

Larry appeared to be growing more and more puzzled by Thomas's account of the deer, and at the last he shook his head. "You're right about that – it's not normal. I don't hunt deer myself, but I know enough about it to realize they are very nervous creatures, especially this time of year when the hunters are after them." He narrowed his eyes thoughtfully. "What do you think it is?"

Thomas shrugged. "I really don't know. I spoke with one of my members who is an experienced hunter, and he said it sounded like they were almost tranquilized, but who would tranquilize a bunch of wild deer, and why?"

Larry looked as though he were about to answer, when there was a knock and Sharon's face peered around the slightly opened door. "Hey, you two – got any drinks for some thirsty ladies out here?"

"Oh, I forgot to ask what Esther wants," Larry started, but Sharon stopped him.

"Diet soda, what else?" she said with a grin.

The decaf coffee was ready, so the two men carried out the coffee carafe, the tea mugs, cream, sugar, and a diet soda poured over ice, all loaded onto two trays. Sharon went back into the kitchen, shaking her head and making "tsk-tsk" noises, and returned shortly with a plate laden with small shortbread cookies, as well as the fruit tray.

"There! Now we're set," she said as she settled onto the sofa with her coffee.

"How is Deanna doing with the new faces, Amy?" Larry asked. Esther got up, brought Deanna over and handed the baby to her father. "Here you go, Dad. You get to see for yourself."

Deanna looked up at Larry and pouted for a few seconds, but after a few worrying seconds settled down without any protests. Larry looked at his daughter with an expression of triumph.

"See? I didn't scare her after all!" Esther giggled, and Larry looked at Amy and Thomas. "She's been warning me all afternoon that I would scare Deanna into conniptions when she saw me. Disrespectful little wretch!"

Esther stuck out her tongue at her father and settled back into the chair with her soda, feet once again tucked up under her.

"How do you like the rooibos tea, Thomas? It's full of antioxidants, and it's a great relaxing drink before you go to bed at night. Very soothing. I'm a pharmacist - I know these things." Larry raised his eyebrows at Thomas, and made a slight nod toward Esther.

"Yeah. It is soothing. I bet I'll have no problem sleeping tonight." He looked over at Esther. "Esther, I'd like to ask a favor of you. I'm curious about some things I've seen lately, and I think you might know something that would help me. It's about the deer in the pasture across from the church, and anything Eddie may have told you about them."

Esther looked at Thomas with huge, brown eyes that shined with unshed tears, but she nodded. "Amy said you are trying to help the police find out who... who..." and she gulped, wiping at her eyes.

Sharon started to get up, but Esther waved her back into her seat. "It's OK, Mom. I've got to get through this, and if I can do something to help bring this person in, the one who did this, then I want to do it." She sipped her soda automatically. "The lady detective that came here on Friday was – oh, I don't know – she just didn't seem to care, you know? It was like it was all just another day to her."

Thomas was sincere when he said, "Esther, I'm truly sorry this happened to Eddie, and for all the pain it has caused you and everyone else who loved Eddie. And I feel an obligation to try to help find out who did this. Not for revenge, though. I want to stop this person from doing something this horrible again. Once you have stepped over that line of killing someone, it becomes easier. Whoever it is, is dangerous to everyone around them."

Esther sat there for a moment, turning the glass in her hands, little drips of condensation from it glistening in the lamp light. Then she said, "About the deer... Eddie was anti-hunting you know? He thought it was inhumane and cruel, for a lot of reasons I won't go into now. Well, he was over there at Mr.

Rothstein's farm one day for some reason – dropping off a package or something. Anyway, he saw the deer in the pasture, and he thought they were just beautiful.

"He walked over to the fence and they seemed to be unafraid of him. He always had a way with animals, but he said this was just weird. It was like they had no clue how dangerous humans could be."

Thomas nodded. "I've experienced that with those deer myself lately. They seem to be either fearless or tame."

"Yeah, well, he heard some of the boys talking at school about deer hunting, and then one of them said he had a friend who was going to shoot a couple 'real easy'. They said it would be like shooting at targets instead of at live deer. Eddie asked around, and listened, and found out they were talking about the deer in that pasture.

"He brought some of his anti-hunting flyers to school and tried to give them out, but the other boys just laughed at him. He even tried to talk to the boys who said they were thinking of going out to shoot those 'tame deer', and they got mad at him, told him he was a jerk and a sissy and all kinds of things."

Thomas said slowly, "So, Eddie decided to take things into his own hands, and go out to the pasture and scare the deer away when someone tried to spotlight them?"

Esther wiped her eyes with her napkin. "Yes. He went and parked on a side road, and would sit in the woods on the nights when he thought they were going to be there. He couldn't always be there, but he messed up their shots a couple of times. And since his parents were out of town on a vacation..." she shrugged and looked down at her hands.

"He was able to be out late at night without anyone questioning him," Larry finished for her.

Esther just nodded.

"What else did Eddie say about the deer, Esther?" Thomas asked. "Did he ever say why he thought they were so docile?"

She sat and thought for a moment. "Well, he was always saying how fat they were. I mean, more than usual. They were either very well-fed or they just ate a lot." She bit her finger, thinking hard. "And he said they were sort of... dreamy, you know?

"They didn't seem to be nervous at all. Deer are usually twitching their ears, their tails. These were just standing there, happy with eating, and they even let him pet them sometimes." She looked up at Thomas, then at her parents, tears on her cheeks. "He loved animals. He would tell me the next day about how cool it was, how wonderful, to be able to touch and feel the life in wild animals like that."

Sharon went over and knelt on the floor by her daughter, hugging her tightly.

No one said anything for a while, then Thomas nervously cleared his throat. "Esther, can I ask a couple more questions? I'm sorry, but these are things that we need to know."

She nodded, wiping her face with a tissue given to her by Sharon. "I'm OK, Thomas. What else do you want to know?"

"Did anyone ever threaten Eddie? I mean, a serious threat, not a joke?" he asked.

She made a sound of disgust, then answered, "Brian Benson, my ex-boyfriend, never threatened him to his face. But he said to me that he would like to kill Eddie, that he would get rid of anyone that stood between us – between Brian and me."

Larry and Thomas looked at each other, then Thomas asked quietly, "Anyone else?"

Esther thought for a few moments, then shook her head. "Nobody I can remember. I mean, he did make all those boys mad with the things he was saying about deer hunters being inhumane and cowards because they used weapons to kill animals that couldn't fight back, but I never heard any of them threatening him."

"Thanks. I think this next question will be pretty much the last one for right now. That night, the night of the play, did you see anyone near the glass Eddie drank from, who wouldn't ordinarily be there?"

Esther's face crinkled in a frown as she strove to remember. "I'm trying to... let's see, on that side of the stage, there was Randy, who played William Blore; Trey, who played Dr. Armstrong, and Daniel, who played Judge Wargrave. But I don't remember if any of them were particularly close to the glass, or the bottle."

Then she looked up at the others. "But it couldn't have been the bottle! Everyone had drinks from the bottle, so it had to be the glass."

"Was there any way anyone could have known which glass would be used by each actor, earlier in the play or before it?" Thomas asked.

"I don't think so," Esther replied. "That's a long, single-scene act, but there are a lot of points when people enter and leave the stage. I guess... well, it would have to have been after the point when Janet – she played the cook, Mrs. Rogers? It would have to have been after she came on and had her long talk onstage with Mr. Rogers. She picked up all the glasses that were sitting around and took them offstage on a tray."

Thomas nodded, satisfied. "That narrows it down. Tell me, do you still have your script from the play?"

"Sure. Why? Do you need it?"

"It would help. Could you get it for me, and mark the names of the students who played each part, and mark the point in the first act where you say it would needed to have been after, for me?"

She arose and went upstairs.

Thomas looked at Larry and Sharon. "I really want to thank you both for letting me impose on you like this. These answers she has given are helping me to get a much clearer picture of what happened.

"I'm not the police, and I don't claim to be. I'm a minister. But a minister is supposed to be dedicated to the truth, and to helping those who are without help. Well, here the truth is being hidden, and someone is getting away with having killed a young man." He grimaced and continued.

"And I have to admit, it hurts me that it happened right there in front of me – both the time someone shot at Eddie, and when he was poisoned. If I can help bring his murderer to justice, then I feel like I will be doing God's will in this."

Larry smiled. "In Judaism, it's called a *mitzvah*. It's when you do a good thing for someone, because you know it's the right thing to do rather than because it's what you have to do or because you get rewarded for it."

Esther came down the stairs with her copy of the script, and handed it to Thomas, who stood to take it.

"Here, I've marked in the names of all the players. And I wrote in the names of the director and anyone who was working backstage, too. Thought you might want that sort of information, too," Esther said. Her eyes were moist, but her mouth was set in a firm line. "I want to know who did this to Eddie."

"I'm not doing this for revenge, Esther," Thomas said quietly.

But Esther just looked at him, turned around and went back upstairs. "Larry, Sharon..." he began.

"Don't worry, Thomas. I know what you meant. And, deep inside, Esther understands too. She is not a vengeful person, but she is hurting right now," Larry said as he and Sharon walked Thomas and Amy to the door.

Amy hugged Sharon. "We'll be praying for all three of you."

Sharon smiled at Amy. "And we will be praying for you three, as well. Shalom."

On the drive home, with Deanna sleeping in her carrier that was safely buckled in, Amy looked at the script laying in her lap. "Do you intend to investigate all these people yourself?" she softly asked her husband.

Thomas was quiet for a few seconds, seeming to concentrate on the road before him. "Amy, I've told you already - I'm not a detective, and I don't want to be. But the truth needs to be discovered, and if I can help do that, then I believe I am doing God's will."

"And what if you endanger yourself in the process?"

"I have to put my trust in God, Amy. He will protect me – I have to believe that." Thomas focused on a car turning in front of him. "And so do you."

Chapter 10

Give not sleep to thine eyes, nor slumber to thine eyelids. Deliver thyself as a roe from the hand of the hunter, and as a bird from the hand of the fowler.
Proverbs 6:4,5

Thomas stood by the window with a cup of coffee, looking outside at the mist rising from the lawn and the pasture across the road. A Jeep drove by and turned in, which he recognized as belonging to Mr. Rothstein. This didn't surprise him, as he had seen him at least a couple of times driving up onto the field.

Rothstein got out and opened the gate, driving through it, across the field and over the top of the hill. He left the gate open.

Soon a second Jeep drove up, a very nice customized job, and also turned in at the gate, following the same track over the hill. Within the next ten minutes, there were four more vehicles that turned in. All were four-wheel-drive vehicles. Two were Range Rovers, and one was a very shiny black Hummer. The last was another Jeep, rusty and not as well maintained as the other vehicles. All of them proceeded over the hill, but the driver of the last Jeep stopped and closed the gate before following the others.

This little parade of vehicles amazed Thomas, as he had never seen anyone in the field other than Mr. Rothstein. Further, the expensive nature of four of them was very impressive. It was like an executive board meeting was being held in Mr. Rothstein's back pasture!

Thomas shook his head and went to the phone. No matter what was going on across the hill, he had to get on with the tasks ahead of him. Thomas gave Eric a call and briefed him on what he had learned from Esther. Eric wasn't in a very good mood, and grunted in response to most of what Thomas told him.

After hanging up, Thomas wondered why Eric was in such a lousy mood, but figured it was because of the pressure of the murder investigation coupled with the investigation of all the break-ins.

Thomas went to his office in the church to prepare for the midweek Bible study and prayer meeting service. He was copying some note-taking sheets, when he heard a distant gunshot, then another. Thomas dashed away, leaving the copier spitting out copies and ran to the front door of the church.

There was no one in the road, no vehicle was stopped. It didn't seem to be the poachers. As Thomas walked out into the parking area and looked around, another shot rang out. The sound came from across the road, and seemed to be from over the hill on the far side of the pasture. Now Thomas knew what was going on with the vehicles that had been turning in at the gate – it must have been a group of hunters.

He looked up at the sky and frowned. It was very late in the morning to be hunting deer, though – almost 10:45 AM. All that he knew about deer hunting held that you got up early and sat waiting for the deer to come feed with the first light of day. Shrugging, he turned and headed back into the church. He wasn't a confirmed deer hunter himself, so maybe this was some different technique.

He finished preparations for the evening's Bible study and decided to go back to the parsonage and see about some lunch.

As he was going out the door, he heard an engine across the road. He turned to see the large black Hummer, this time with a tarp-wrapped bundle tied atop it, on the luggage rack. It was followed by one of the Range Rovers, which also had a bundle tied to the luggage rack.

The owner of the Range Rover had not done such a good job with the wrapping of the tarp, however. As the Range Rover drove by, Thomas glimpsed a huge set of antlers protruding from beneath the blue tarp. Thomas stopped in amazement as two more vehicles came out of the field and turned onto the roadway, all with similar blue-wrapped bundles tied to their luggage racks. Now that Thomas had a good idea of what was inside the tarps, the outlines of the antlers were easy to discern.

At last Mr. Rothstein's Jeep and the older Jeep came over the hill. As Thomas watched from the front of the church, the driver of the more battered vehicle stopped after both he and Rothstein passed out the gate, and shut the gate, locking it.

Rothstein eased out from the drive, and Thomas waved in a friendly way to him as he passed the church. There was no answering wave, however, only what Thomas would have sworn looked to be a glare from the owner of the pasture.

After lunch, Thomas once again turned to Stan Bowman for help with questions about deer hunting. When Stan answered the phone, Thomas said, "Stan, this is Pastor Wilson. I know I'll probably see you tonight at church, but something has me puzzled. I've got another question or two about deer and deer hunting."

Stan laughed. "Pastor, you know, we ought to just borrow a gun from someone and take you out with us, so you can see how it's done! But, until then, what can I help you with?"

"Remember those deer I told you about, the ones that are so docile?"

115

"The ones across the road in the pasture, right?"

"Right. Well, this morning, the owner of the property across the road had a hunting party over there or something. He had at least four or five vehicles besides his own that followed him across the pasture and over that hill, and they look to have shot at least four large deer. And these had impressive sets of antlers, too!"

"That's not all that unusual, pastor, for someone with a lot of property to invite their friends or business acquaintances to hunt on their land. They must have had mighty good luck!" Stan paused. "But how did you happen to be up so early, to catch them all going over to get set up for the hunt."

"Well, that was another odd thing. They didn't drive over into the field until, oh, well after 8:30 this morning. And they shot the deer between 10:30 and 11:00. I heard all the gunshots."

Now it was Stan's turn to be puzzled. "They were driving into the hunting area at 8:30 AM?"

"Or a little later, yes."

"That's pretty strange. It's usual for the deer to be really spooked by this point in the season, and the sound of four or five vehicles driving into their territory should have pushed them farther into the woods to bed down. And to shoot the deer so late in the day... How many did you say they shot?"

"It looked to be four, from the bundles going out on top of the vehicles," Thomas answered.

"Well, if they killed all four within that small space of time, the deer couldn't have been too spooked!" Stan's voice held a note of skepticism as well as puzzlement. "Something doesn't sound right, pastor. Sounds like the hunt was very well planned – maybe too well planned."

"What do you mean?"

"Well, last year there was a big stink about a fellow in another state who had some deer penned up in a small area – about 5 acres. The deer were all prime specimens. They were raised on farms from fawns, and fed the best feed. This made them beautiful animals – and almost tame.

"After they got to be trophy size, this person would sell 'hunts' to people who were rich enough to come there to his place and who wanted to kill a trophy buck without having to go to the trouble of finding one."

"You mean they would just come out and shoot tame deer in an enclosure? That's not hunting – that's just slaughtering an animal!" Thomas was shocked. "And these 'hunters' go home and hang the head of the deer they kill this way on their walls and call it a trophy?"

"Exactly. Disgusting, isn't it? And it's illegal. Well, at least most places it's illegal. It's illegal in this state, that's for sure! You think that might be what was happening across the road?"

Thomas was hesitant. "I don't know. I know that the four vehicles that came out with deer tied on top of them were very nice, expensive vehicles. I couldn't have afforded any of them!" Thomas thought. "And you know, at least one of them had an out-of-state tag. I remember noticing it on the black Hummer that drove by."

"Well, if he is holding that kind of 'captive hunting' over there, it's no wonder he was nervous about you, or anyone else, wandering around in his pasture. He wouldn't want anyone discovering what he was doing," Stan stated. "Like I said, it's illegal in this state."

"Do you think he could be doing that?" Thomas asked. Mr. Rothstein had seemed too ordinary and business-like to be involved in such shady dealings.

"I don't know much about Charles Rothstein, pastor," Stan said. "But I do know that he has four or five businesses in the area, and that he's a wealthy man by local standards. If he did have a captive hunt, it could be for profit. There are people willing to pay a pretty penny for a trophy buck without the trouble of tracking it down or sitting in a deer stand for hours.

"Or, it could be as a sort of business incentive – you know, like taking a good customer out on a deep-sea fishing trip or something like that. Of course, that's for profit too, in the long run."

"I suppose you're right. I appreciate your insight," Thomas said.

"Not at all, pastor. Glad to help. Tell me, do you think this has anything to do with the murder of that boy?"

Startled, Thomas said, "No, not that I can see! Why? How could it"

Stan drew a deep breath. "Pastor, you are a good man, but sometimes you are a little naive. Suppose you had arranged a little 'party' for a group of business associates, that would assure a steady flow of business and money from those folks if it went well. Hundreds of thousands of dollars in business, maybe more. Would you want to take the chance that some anti-hunting do-gooder would blow it all for you, and maybe get you in trouble with the law into the bargain?"

Thomas's hand gripped the phone tighter. "I see what you mean, Stan. I hadn't thought of it from that angle." He paused, then continued. "I'll see you tonight at midweek service, then?"

"I'll be there, pastor."

"Good. Take care, and thanks again." Thomas hung up. After staring out the window at the now deserted pasture across the road, he decided to call Eric again. He dialed the number, but got only Eric's voice mail. He left a message for Eric to call him when he returned, then hung up.

His own phone rang just then, and when he answered it was one of his church members.

"Teresa, how are you?"

"I'm fine, pastor, but Jack isn't doing well. He injured himself at work today and is at the emergency room now. I'm stuck here at home because I'm watching my own kids plus two more." There was a note of pleading and urgency in her voice. "I can't take four kids down there to the emergency room, and he isn't supposed to drive himself home. Do you think..."

"Don't you worry. Would you like me to go and see about getting Jack home this afternoon?"

"Pastor, that would be wonderful if you could. They drove his car to the ER for him, but he won't be able to drive it home."

"I'll get Amy to drop me off at the hospital, and I'll drive Jack home, then Amy can come and get me at your house."

Teresa Fox sounded grateful but worried. "Pastor, that is a lot for you to do! I feel bad for asking, but..."

"Hush, Teresa! Not another word. It's another chance for me to get a blessing out of helping one of my wonderful and supportive members! Now go and take care of those kids," he said, because he could hear children playing and yelling in the background.

"Thanks, pastor!" she said and hung up.

Thomas and Amy drove to the hospital, with Deanna murmuring and making baby noises in the backseat. He told Amy all about what Stan Bowman shared with him regarding the possible happenings in the pasture across the road.

Amy shook her head at the idea. "Thomas, I'll eat venison, but these people who shoot a deer just for the purpose of collecting a head for their wall disgust me. And to do it that way, with a captive herd, is the lowest form of hunting sportsmanship! But do you believe that's what Mr. Rothstein did over there?"

"I don't know, Amy. I can't say, because I wasn't there. But it sure is suspicious – the deer that are so complacent and friendly, the group of high-end four-by-fours disappearing over the hill, followed by four shots within moments of each other, and then those same four vehicles driving out of the pasture with large trophy bucks wrapped in tarps and lashed to their luggage racks."

"Thomas, you only saw one that you can say with certainty was a deer," Amy reminded him.

"True, but the rest of them... well, if they weren't deer, why were they shaped like deer and why were they wrapped up the same way as the one that *was* a deer?" Thomas said in a very convincing manner.

Amy had no answer for that. Soon they arrived at the hospital, and Amy let Thomas out to go into the Emergency Room. He leaned in and kissed her. "I'll call you when I know any details, or if anything changes. I have to get back to the parsonage this afternoon, anyway. We have service tonight." Amy drove away as Thomas entered the hospital.

Jack Fox was in one of the small, curtained-off rooms used for emergency room patients. He sat on a gurney, with his right forearm wrapped in an abundance of Ace bandage.

"Jack, what have you been up to? Your wife said you were injured at work," Thomas said as he walked in.

Jack Fox looked at Thomas with surprise. "Pastor! I didn't expect to see you here. Did Teresa call you?"

Thomas nodded. "Yes, she did. She is babysitting a total of four kids today, it seems, and she didn't want to try to bring that thundering herd here to the Emergency Room."

Jack's eyes grew wider. "I'd forgotten about that. And they won't let me drive home, although I do have my car here."

"So, I'm going to drive you home when they release you, and Amy is going to come and pick me up from your house," Thomas finished for him.

Jack Fox frowned. "That's a lot of trouble, pastor. I can get a taxi..." but Thomas cut him off.

"Not at all. Remember earlier this year when I was laid up from the car accident? All you brethren of the church were lined up to take me anywhere I needed to go! That's a two-way street, you know," Thomas said with a smile. "How are you feeling, anyway? And what happened?"

Jack looked down at his arm. "Well, with the painkillers in me, and my arm immobilized, I guess I'm feeling alright. By tomorrow morning, though, it may not be so pleasant." He grinned at the pastor.

"As for what happened," he continued, "you know where I work, right? The big carpet factory, Olson's?" Thomas nodded, and Jack went on, "Well, I'm one of the floor managers there, so I go around two or three times a day at least, checking on how things are going, making sure jobs are getting finished, that sort of thing."

He grimaced. "We have a 'Drugs Don't Work Here' policy, but every now and then someone will slip through the net of urine tests and such that we do when we hire people. I guess I'm here because of one of the slippery ones."

Thomas cocked his head sideways, looking at Jack. "How's that?"

"I went out onto the loading dock today, and was making sure things were going OK out there. We've had a couple of trucks lately to come up at the far end of the delivery with the wrong carpet on them, so I was double-checking things. I had just gotten through checking this one trailer and stepped out of it, when a Hyster came around the corner at full speed, with a roll of carpet sticking out in front of it.

"The driver didn't even seem to see me. He just turned and swatted me with that big roll of carpet. The roll was 12 feet long and almost three feet in diameter, and when he swung it around it hit me like a ball bat – knocked me for a loop. I went over another roll laying on the dock, and ended up breaking my wrist." He looked down at his bandage-encased arm and wriggled his fingers, wincing at the effect.

"The driver of the Hyster was on drugs?" Thomas asked, dumbfounded.

"Not hard drugs probably, but my company does a urine, breathalyzer or blood test as a matter of policy whenever a Hyster accident occurs. He wasn't drunk, but he was sure high. They could tell that, so the company security searched his locker and found two small bags of marijuana. They figure his blood test will come back positive, too, but they have to wait for that."

"I've never experienced marijuana, or even been around anyone who is smoking it," said Thomas. "I guess I'm a little inexperienced in that sort of thing. What made you, or security, guess that he was high?"

Jack shifted on the gurney, easing his arm by putting a pillow under it. "Well, I don't know how pot affects everybody, but this guy was just drowsy looking – very laid-back, very relaxed. His eyes were bloodshot. And he didn't even seem to be upset by the fact that he almost knocked me into next week, or that they found the pot in his locker. He just said, 'Oh, sorry, Mr. Fox.'"

"How old is this Hyster driver?" Thomas asked.

"He's 23. We don't let anyone under 21 drive a Hyster. It's not a state law, but company policy. The company used to let 18-year-old kids drive them, but they caught them having races during the third shift a couple of times, so they fired those kids and made a rule that only employees 21 and older could drive them. They have to complete a safety course, too." Jack Fox snorted. "I don't think this guy remembered what he learned there."

Thomas smiled. "I guess not. Well, thank God he didn't do more damage."

Jack nodded soberly. "I know. We had a man killed a few years ago. You know, those Hysters that carry the carpet rolls have long steel pipes with tapered tips on them, to slip into the roll and lift them from the racks. They're like six-inch-thick nails, fourteen feet long.

"A driver was driving too fast, and he came around a corner, lost control of his machine and pinned a man to a wall through the abdomen. The pole went all the way through the man, and halfway through the concrete block wall. He died on the way to the hospital," Jack said, with a very solemn look on his face.

"We have rules that say the poles are always supposed to be at ground level when the driver has the machine in motion from point A to point B, but this person was in a hurry and didn't pay attention."

A nurse came in at that point, checked Jack's arm, and must have been satisfied with it. She gave Jack a prescription for some painkillers, and sent him on his way.

While Jack paid the ER bill, Thomas called Amy and told her he was about to leave for Jack's house. She would meet him there and take him back to the parsonage.

They stopped to allow Jack to fill his prescription, so by the time they arrived at the Fox residence, Amy was already there, and she and Teresa were playing with Deanna. The father of the two children Teresa watched had just left with his kids, so Teresa was beginning to wind down.

Everyone went inside for a few minutes, and Teresa thanked Thomas for bringing Jack home. "With the broken wrist, plus the pain killers, there's no way he would have been able to drive home."

Jack looked at the bottle of medicine he held in his hand. "Pastor, I hope you'll understand if I don't show up for the service tonight. After I take one of these, I bet I'll be more mellow and laid back than the stupid guy who ran into me with the carpet! I don't want to start snoring in the middle of Bible study."

Thomas laughed. "I'll explain to everyone where you are, Jack, and we'll have special prayer for your speedy recovery. Get well quickly, you hear?"

They left then, and Amy drove them home to the parsonage. Thomas was very quiet on the way, sifting things through his mind, thinking about all the things he had heard and seen for the last couple of days. *Could it be... no, he wouldn't do that... would he?*

Chapter 11

An unjust man is an abomination to the just: and he that is upright in the way is abomination to the wicked.
Psalms 29:27

The evening service was well-attended – at least for a midweek service – and people were suitably concerned and empathetic over Jack Fox's reported injury. After the service, the Ladies Auxiliary decided to bake Jack's favorite cake (triple-layer carrot cake) and take it by his house with a card and some flowers, which made Thomas chuckle.

Stan Bowman came by while Thomas shook hands, and hung around for a few minutes. It was obvious he wanted to talk about something, so when everyone had been given their due handshake and greeting, he and Stan headed toward Thomas's office.

"What's on your mind, Stan?" Thomas asked as they sat down.

"Oh, you just have me curious about the deer in the field, now. I wondered if you had any further ideas, or if you had seen anything more, that's all," Stan replied.

Thomas said, "I haven't had a chance to see the deer any more since we spoke. My trip to pick up Jack and then the service tonight had me pretty well tied up." He didn't want to mention the other thoughts that had been bouncing around inside his head – they just seemed too bizarre.

Stan nodded, but looked disappointed. "I thought that might be the case. You know, I'm a member of a couple of hunting organizations, and I'll put out the word, very discretely, for them to let me know of any recent rumors they may have heard about captive hunting in or around the area. Sometimes people get talkative when they think they're going to bag a big buck – they start bragging in advance, you know?"

"That would be interesting to know! I'm pretty convinced that's what happened over there, but whether it was for money or to curry favor with a business associate, I have no idea," Thomas said.

"And," he added, "my biggest concern at the moment is less those deer than the death of Eddie Kusack. They may be connected, but I'm not sure of that."

Stan nodded, just looking at Thomas for a few moments. Then he said, "I didn't even know you knew the Kusack family, pastor. I don't believe I know them – hadn't even heard of them until this murder was in the papers."

Thomas then told Stan about he play at the synagogue-run high school, and a little bit about his friends, the Meyers family.

Stan listened, then said, "I can understand how you want to help, pastor. No matter what church or religion that kid belonged to, it was a rotten thing to poison him, and dangerous to the other kids, as well. If I can help, let me know." He stood up, but turned to Thomas as he was about to leave. "Just remember, though, that there may be people in the church who won't be happy about you in the role of detective." They walked to the church foyer, where Amy waited with Deanna in her arms.

"Deanna's getting hungry, Thomas, and I wasn't sure where you were. I'm going on over to the parsonage and feed her, alright? Oh, and good night, Stan," she said as she turned and went out the door.

Thomas turned out all the lights and locked the church, then jogged behind Amy to the parsonage, catching up with her just in time to open the door for her. He held Deanna while Amy prepared her late dinner, and they sat and talked while the baby enjoyed her bottle.

"You know, Amy, I've been wondering about something," Thomas began, then stopped, eyes unfocused as he looked down at Deanna. Amy looked at him, then nudged him with her elbow as he stayed silent.

"Wondering about what? Wondering how long it will be before Deanna stops taking a bottle?" she teased him.

Thomas reached over and touched his daughter's face with a forefinger, then shook his head. "No, that's not a problem for me. I like holding her and feeding her, when I get the chance."

Whereupon Amy extended Deanna and bottle to Thomas, who took them both with a smile. He resumed feeding her just in time to stop her complaint at the pause in food, and said, "Actually, it's about the deer across the road, and sort of odd, and I'd like to bounce it off you and see what you think."

Amy nodded. "OK, tell me about it."

"Stan Bowman told me about how his wrist was broken at the carpet mill where he works, and that's what started me thinking about this. A Hyster driver…"

"What's a Hyster?" Amy asked.

"Ah, sorry. A Hyster is a very heavy, small wheeled vehicle that is used to lift and move heavy loads, like pallets full of stuff, or, in this case, rolls of carpet," Thomas explained.

"So, anyway, this Hyster driver was carrying a big roll of carpet around on a pole that sticks out from the front of the Hyster, and he came around a corner very fast. The roll of carpet swung around and just knocked Stan over another roll that laying there on the loading dock floor."

"Ouch!" Amy exclaimed. "What was the driver thinking?"

"That's just it – he appears to have been under the influence of drugs. He acted very relaxed, very unconcerned, and they found two bags of pot in his locker. Of course, they took a blood sample, too, and that will be tested to make sure. But they think he had been smoking marijuana, which impaired his judgment and made him too relaxed to respond the way he should have."

Deanna made some aggravated noises, and Thomas looked down. He saw that the bottle was empty, so he lifted Deanna and burped her against his shoulder.

"But, what does all that have to do with the deer in the pasture, Thomas?" Amy asked, taking Deanna from him.

"I'm getting to that part. Remember how Jack said today that, if he took one of those pain pills, he would be as mellow and relaxed as the guy who hit him with the carpet?"

"Yess-s-s," Amy replied, curiosity in her eyes.

"Well, that made me wonder. If the drugs could make Jack all relaxed and mellow, and if the pot-smoking Hyster driver was so relaxed and unconcerned with what might happen – could that be why the deer in the pasture are so unwary, even to the point of letting someone stand in the middle of them and pet them?"

Amy's brow furrowed. "You mean, someone is putting drugs in their feed or something like that?"

"Something like that, yes."

Amy rolled her eyes, looking at Thomas with mild skepticism. "Do you really think Mr. Rothstein is doping up deer to make them easier to shoot?"

Thomas blushed. "Well, when you say it out loud, it does seem sort of silly."

"Besides, I thought your focus was on finding out who killed Eddie, not how the deer were getting poached," Amy reminded him.

Thomas turned and poured himself a cup of coffee, then sat down at the table. He was silent for a few minutes, then said, "I know you're right, that I do want to find out who killed Eddie. But somehow, I have the feeling that these two are tied together. Remember, someone shot at Eddie in the field that night."

"You can't be sure of that, Thomas. You only think they may have shot at Eddie. You didn't see them aim, whoever this unknown 'they' may be," Amy said, sitting down across from him with her own cup of coffee.

Breathing a deep sigh, Thomas nodded in acknowledgement. "I know, Amy. But I sure would like to talk this over with Eric. Maybe I'll drop by there tomorrow morning."

Amy stood up and took the sleeping Deanna in her carrier. "I'm putting this little one to bed, Thomas, and I think you need to get to bed, too. Your eyes look very tired and bloodshot. You can't think when you're short of sleep, you know." She leaned down and kissed him. "See you in a little while."

Thomas sat at the table for a little while, thinking. Who would poison Eddie Kusack, and why? For that matter, where would they get the poison? Brian Benson had a motive. Maybe Charles Rothstein had a motive. Was there anyone else? He shook his head, and then a thought crossed his mind.

Thomas got up and went into the den where they kept a computer he used for communicating with others by E-mail, as well as for taking the occasional online theological course. He dialed into the Internet, and used an online search engine to look up "sodium cyanide." In a few seconds, he had a listing of over 790,000 hits. Taking a deep breath, he decided he needed to narrow his search a little. He typed in "Sodium cyanide, uses". On the fourth page of the listing, he found an article that made his eyes open wide.

* * *

The next morning, Thomas got up very early. He went over to the church as usual to pray and read the Bible. He especially desired God's wisdom today, so his prayers were even more fervent than usual.

He returned to the house, kissed Amy and Deanna, and drove downtown to the police station. There, he found that Detective Eric Lamonde had just gotten out of a meeting, and he didn't look all that happy.

"Eric, can I see you for a few minutes?" Thomas asked hesitantly.

Eric looked at him for a few seconds, then motioned for Thomas to follow him into his office, where he shut the door.

"Thomas, you're a friend, but right now I'd love to have a good, long swear, and I simply can't do it with you sitting there." He leaned back in his chair and ran his hands across the top of his head, ruffling his short-cropped hair. "What can I do for you, though?"

Thomas smiled apologetically. "Sorry, Eric – I don't mean to cramp your style. Want me to go and get some coffee while you curse?"

Eric snorted. "No, and you know it! Seriously, what can I do for you?"

"I have a couple of questions, and maybe I can help you a little," Thomas said. He opened the small briefcase he had brought with him. "Here are some things for you, though. I wrote down notes from the conversation I had with Esther Meyers the other night, as well as other information I got from her father." He slid the sheets across the desk to Eric.

Eric picked them up and read them with interest. "You mean, she told you that Eddie really was able to get into the field and touch the deer, that they didn't run from him?"

"It corroborates my story about someone standing in the field and petting the deer, too. And they didn't act afraid of me, either, Eric." Thomas reminded him about the experience of tossing the rock and then yelling at the deer, and how they had seemed to be without any fear.

Eric frowned. "But that doesn't make sense, unless these were tame deer. Pets, you know?"

"Well, I have a theory about that…"

"Let me finish reading these notes, Thomas," Eric said, and scanned the rest of the page.

He looked up again. "So, the Benson boy did make a threat against Eddie," he said with some satisfaction. "That is a good start. Combine that with a motive, and it could be helpful to us." He continued reading.

"And the reason Kusack went to that field is because he heard these boys at school talking about how the deer in that field would be so easy to shoot… and he was an anti-hunting activist," Eric mumbled as he read.

At last he looked up. "Thanks for including the list of the actors in the play. We already had that information, though."

Thomas leaned forward and tapped his finger on the page. "But do you see those top three names? Those are the kids who were closest to the glass Eddie drank from, right before it happened."

Eric's eyes widened. "Well, well. We didn't have THAT information. Thanks, Thomas."

Thomas cleared his throat. "I have something else, though. You may have already thought of it, but I thought I'd tell you, anyway."

Eric waited without saying anything, so Thomas continued. "You said it was sodium cyanide that killed Eddie, right?"

"That's what the coroner says," Eric answered.

"Sodium cyanide – well, it's used for a few different things, and last night I got curious, so I looked it up on the Internet," Thomas said.

Eric laughed. "I didn't know you were an Internet geek, Thomas!"

Thomas chuckled. "I'm not, but I do use it when I think it's useful. Anyway, when I did a search on uses for sodium cyanide, I found something very interesting. It's used for, among other things, plating metal. Electroless plating with gold, in fact."

Eric looked puzzled. "OK, so it's used in gold plating. Is that supposed to be important?"

"Remember I told you that Charles Rothstein owns the property where the deer were?"

"Yeah, I remember."

"And remember that someone took a potshot at Eddie that night…"

"You *think* someone took a potshot at Eddie," Eric said.

"Yes, I do think that. I think that, maybe, Charles Rothstein had a good reason for not wanting anyone poking around on his property."

"What reason would that be, other than wanting to keep trespassers off his land?" Eric asked.

"I think he has been preparing those tame deer for a captive shoot, maybe by doping them, and that's why they were so tame."

Eric laughed, then stopped as he saw that Thomas didn't even have a smile. "You're serious?" he asked.

"Very serious," Thomas answered. Then he told Eric in detail all about the mid-morning hunt and parade of high-dollar four-wheel-drive vehicles, all carrying deer.

"Okay, that MIGHT make for a reason for someone to take a warning shot at someone. But we can't prove it, and we don't have a good reason to investigate Mr. Rothstein, Thomas. The DA would look at us like we are crazy. After all, Rothstein is a wealthy and influential man around here."

"And he owns a lot of businesses…"

"Exactly my point," Eric said, nodding.

"Like that auto customization shop, where they do all sorts of special-order plating – gold hubcaps, that sort of thing."

Eric's next comment died in his mouth, leaving it hanging open. "Do they use sodium cyanide there?" he finally asked.

"I don't know. But I bet your detectives could find out. The coroner might even be able to match it to the stuff that killed Eddie Kusack, if they do," Thomas said.

"I was already thinking that very thing," Eric said. "Thomas, I appreciate all the information you have brought by here today. And now, I just need the time and space to use it to best advantage." He looked pointedly at Thomas as he picked up the phone.

Thomas stood up. "I understand, Eric. Do you still need a good, long swear?"

Eric was already on the phone and speaking with someone, so he just shook his head at Thomas and shooed him out the door.

On the way home from the police station, Thomas decided to drop by Meyers Pharmacy and see how things were going with Esther. Larry had three customers when Thomas first walked in, so he read magazines while he waited. Soon Larry was finished with those customers and he came around the counter after asking his assistant, Ben, to watch things for a few minutes.

"Thomas, how are you?" Larry asked.

"I was going to ask you the same question, and ask you how Esther is doing, too. I was downtown, so I thought I'd drop by and check on you." He put the magazine back in the rack, and he walked with Larry to the back of the store and into a small office there.

"We're all doing pretty well, all things considered. But Esther had something she wanted to tell you when she came home from school yesterday," Larry said as he took a seat.

Thomas sat down, too. "What was it about?"

Larry grimaced. "I wish I knew the details, but I don't. But she was sort of excited. Not 'happy' excited, but like she was on edge about something." He looked at his watch. "She gets home from school at about 3:30. Want me to leave a message there for her to call you?"

"Please do, Larry. I know Esther is very motivated to find a solution to this, and if she has discovered something that might help, I'd like to know about it."

Larry raised a cautionary hand. "Now don't get your hopes up, Thomas. She may just have an idea, or a possibility."

"I know, I know. Still, every little bit can help." And with that, he told Larry in detail about his theory regarding the deer in the pasture, the captive hunt, and the possibility of the deer being doped to increase their docility and make it easier to shoot them.

"So," he finished up, "if Charles Rothstein stood to get in a lot of trouble by doing this, or maybe lose his standing in the community, which could have a catastrophic effect on his businesses, he might be willing to do something drastic."

"Charlie Rothstein?" Larry was shocked, his brow wrinkled with concern and disbelief. "Listen, Thomas, the details may all hang together, but Charlie Rothstein is a very respected guy in this town, and in the synagogue! It's hard to believe he might even fire a warning shot over Eddie's head, much less shoot at him to kill him or, God forbid, try to poison him!"

"Larry, I'm not trying to do a character assassination here. I just want to find out who killed Eddie Kusack! Don't you agree that all the facts do fit, and they point in Rothstein's direction?

Larry started to open his mouth, then closed it again. He drummed his fingers on his desk, shaking his head. As though the words were being pulled from him, he said, "It does look bad for him. It's just…" and he paused. "It's just that, when I first came to this town over twelve years ago, Charlie

Rothstein helped me get started with a loan. I was new here, and had never been a business partner. I couldn't get a bank loan to buy into this business – it used to be Fenton's Pharmacy, did you know that? I bought it out lock, stock and barrel eight years ago." Larry sighed and continued, "I paid him back in five years, of course, but I still feel a sense of obligation to him."

Thomas looked at Larry, and slowly nodded. "I do understand, Larry, and I appreciate your loyalty. But I only want the truth, just as you do."

Larry breathed deeply, and said, "Yes, I want the truth, too. No matter who's guilty, we have to know." He stood up then, and shook himself a little as though to throw off the tension. "Thanks for telling me all about this, Thomas. Really."

Thomas shook his hand, and they went back toward the main area of the store. "I'll give Esther a call about 4:00 if I don't hear from her, is that alright?"

On the drive home, Thomas listened to his favorite Christian radio station, and they were playing some old hymns. As he heard the music, and absorbed the facts behind the words, he began to relax. "Only believe, only believe... all things are possible," went the words to the hymn.

Lord, help me to believe, and lead me to the truth, he prayed as he drove.

Thomas was passing through town, and stopped at a traffic light. The hymn stopped, and an advertisement came on the radio. Thomas looked around, and right across on the opposite corner, was Rothstein Customization – the shop where cars, trucks and motorcycles were turned into glittering works of art. When the light turned green, Thomas made a left-hand turn into their parking lot.

When Thomas opened the door to the shop, loud rock music assailed his ears. Any beginnings of a plausible excuse for being there left his mind, washed away by the waves of sound. But it didn't seem to be a problem. There were several customers in the shop, all examining various accessories for their vehicles, and a few people behind the counter who were very busy.

Thomas poked about in the chrome and stainless steel hubcaps, fuel caps, brake and gas pedal replacements until the horde in the shop thinned somewhat. One of the young men behind the counter, with a name tag that said "Theo", came over and asked if he could help Thomas.

Thomas had recovered some of his wits by now. He turned to the young man, who looked to be about 16, and said, "Yes, I hope so. I wonder – if I wanted to get some hubcaps plated, say in chrome or nickel, you can do that here, right?"

The young man looked at Thomas, then over Thomas's shoulder at the minivan Thomas had parked in front of the shop. There was an air of amused skepticism on Theo's face.

"Well, yes, we could do that. We do chrome, nickel, silver, even gold. We did some platinum once, but that was a special order." Thomas could see the young man was amused at the idea of the minivan with customized hubcaps.

"Ah, I see. Tell me, what sort of process do you use here?" Thomas asked, all wide-eyed innocence.

Theo's brow furrowed. "Process?"

"Yes. Is it electroplating or… you know… electroless?"

"Oh. Well, we do both. The electroless is more expensive, usually," Theo answered.

Thomas nodded. He had found out what he needed, but now what?

"Um, tell me," he asked, "how much would it cost to get the hubcaps on that van out there chrome plated?"

"Well, sir," Theo answered, a grin dancing at the edge of his mouth, "you couldn't. The hubcaps on that van are plastic. All the stock hubcaps on family cars are plastic nowadays. You'd have to either buy some metal hubcaps for it, or buy new wheels." He paused. "I'd go with the new wheels, if it was me."

"Ah, I see," Thomas stumbled. "I guess I need to find out more about my car before I go spending lots of money on it, don't I?"

"Prob'ly a good idea, sir," Theo answered.

"Well, thanks for your help," Thomas said as he turned to leave. As the door closed, he thought he heard whoops of laughter behind him mixed with the blaring rock music, but he didn't want to turn around and look.

Chapter 12

And whatsoever shall seem good to thee, and to thy brethren, to do with the rest of the silver and the gold, that do after the will of your God.

Ezra 7:18

Thomas spent the rest of the afternoon visiting two sick members of his congregation. He arrived home a little after 4:00 PM, and there was a message from Esther on the voice mail, to call her when he got in.

Amy was at one of the infant enrichment classes being held at the community center, so he called Esther as soon as he got the message. Sitting down at his the kitchen table with a note pad, he waited for her to pick up the phone. Just as he was about to give up and call back later, he heard a young voice say, "Hello? I'm here, I'm here!"

It was Esther. She had been feeding their cat, she explained, and didn't hear the phone ring at first because of the can opener.

"How have you been?" Thomas asked.

"Mmmm... pretty good most of the time. It hurts, you know?" Short embarrassed silence, then a cleared throat, and she continued, "Sorry, I don't mean to whine."

"Esther, did I say you sound like a whiner? I don't think that at all. You've been through a terrible experience, seeing the young man you care about die before your eyes, and not being able to do anything about it." He took a deep breath. "It will hurt for a long time. But it will get better, easier to deal with, and you will heal. You just have to have faith and hang in there, and remember that your friends and family are there so you can lean on them."

"I know. That's what Rabbi Leibmann said, too. I've been seeing the school counselor every now and then, but she's stretched pretty thin with everybody that was in the play, as well as some other kids that Eddie's death hit pretty hard." She was quiet again, so Thomas took the initiative.

"Your father said you wanted to tell me something. I assume it's something about all the stuff we're trying to figure out. Is it?"

"Yes. Yes, it is. But I don't know… well, I don't know how helpful it will be."

"Just share it with me, and we can figure out together how helpful it is. How about that?" Thomas suggested.

There was almost quiet on the line, and Thomas could hear Esther's breathing. Then, hesitantly, she began.

"Yesterday, I was sitting outside the Counselor's office, in the waiting area. It was about 10:00 in the morning, and I wanted to see her, 'cause I felt really down. Yesterday was the six-month anniversary of when Eddie and I first went out on a date, and, well…" she made a sniffling sound.

"I understand. Anniversary dates are hard. I get sad every year on the anniversary of my mother's death, so I understand."

"Yeah, well, I'm glad you understand. Anyway, I felt depressed, and was waiting to see Mrs. Terrance. This boy came in, Theodore Rosen, and sat right across from me. He was acting fidgety, like he had to go to the bathroom or something, but the bathrooms are right outside the counselor's office, so that must not have been it.

"Anyway, he looked at me, and it was like he hadn't realized I was even there. He jumped, you know what I mean? Then he looked at me, but he wouldn't look me in the eyes. In a little while, he got up and started to leave.

"Mrs. Terrance came out the door of her office then, and said, 'Theo, do you need me for something?' But he just shook his head and said he remembered he had to go somewhere before he went to his DCT assignment. So, he left, and I went on in to see the counselor."

Thomas was puzzled. There must have been a reason for her to tell him this, but he hadn't caught on yet. So he asked another question. "Esther, what is 'DCT'?"

"Oh, that's a program where a student in grades 11 and 12 can work a job in the afternoons as part of their schoolwork. They get vocational credit for it, and they get paid, too. It's a pretty good deal, if you aren't planning to go to college. You get out of the school, you earn some money and you get graduation credit for it, too."

"Oh, yes! I've heard of that, but I didn't know what it was called."

"I don't know what the initials stand for, either, Reverend Wilson." Then she was silent, as though waiting for him to ask another question.

"Okay, I'm going to have to sound stupid here, Esther. I think it must be obvious to you why this is significant to me, but I'm missing something. Who is this boy, Theodore Rosen?"

"He was in the play. Do you remember the names I wrote down for you? He wasn't an actor, but he helped with the setup of the scenery, the between-scenes changes, that sort of thing."

A light went on in Thomas's head. "Yes, I remember reading the name. He was the property master, right?"

Esther giggled. "Well, I guess you could say that. It was his job to scrape together anything weird that we needed for the set – like cigarette boxes, old lamps, serving trays – all that sort of stuff. And like I said, he helped with the scene changes, too."

"But what was significant about this to you, Esther?"

"Theodore Rosen and Eddie didn't get along. Theo was a sort of 'redneck', if you can picture a Jewish redneck. He didn't like the things Eddie was saying about hunting, and I think he was jealous, too. You see, he read for the part of Anthony Marston, but he didn't get it. Eddie did."

"So you're thinking he might be the one who…"

"Reverend Wilson, he had lots of opportunities. He set up the props on the stage, and he was there between scenes. He didn't like Eddie at all. And he acted very weird when he sat across from me – like I said, he couldn't look me in the eye."

Now another small light began to glow in the back of Thomas's mind. "Esther, can you describe this boy to me?"

"Sure. Dark hair, brown eyes, but some freckles. He keeps his hair cut pretty short. He tries to grow a mustache, but it doesn't work very well. About 5'10" or so."

Thomas's internal light bulb glowed brighter. "And his name is Theo?"

"His friends call him that, but his name is Theodore," Esther replied.

In his mind, Thomas saw the amused young man in the customization shop. The name tag read "Theo".

"Do you know where Theodore works, Esther?"

"I think it's a body shop or a garage, because he's always talking about working on cars, trucks and motorcycles," she replied. "Like I said, he's a sort of Jewish redneck. And he's good with tools, which is why he was so handy with the scenery and stuff. He built some of the stuff we used on the set."

"Esther, thank you very much for telling me all this. It might be very useful, but I'll have to talk to Detective Lamonde about it. He's the one with the official authority, you know? And if you remember anything else, anything at all, please feel free to go ahead and call me. Or if you want, you can E-mail me. My E-mail address is *pastorthomas@hccc.org.*

"Okay, Reverend Wilson. I'll be sure to either phone you or E-mail you if anything else comes up," Esther promised.

"Thanks, Esther. You really are a very big help in this!" he said, and they hung up.

Thomas sat there, his mind cluttered with thoughts. What was this? A new complication? A new suspect? He was getting into very deep waters now.

Thomas sat and looked out the window, brooding a little. This was getting worse and worse, he thought. How am I supposed to see, how am I supposed to discern, who did this? He drummed his finger on his desk, then knelt beside his chair.

Father, I need some guidance here. I don't want to accuse the wrong person of anything. I need help, Lord.

The ringing doorbell interrupted his prayer. When Thomas answered the door, he was surprised to see Simon Daniels standing there.

"Simon, come in! What brings you by? Has there been some sort of problem out at the church site?" Thomas asked as he led Simon into the den and they sat down.

"No, just haven't seen you for a couple of days, other than at church, so I thought I'd drop by and see how things are goin' for you." He fidgeted a little. "Fact is, I was curious about how things are goin' for you with the investigation."

Thomas took a deep breath. "I wish I could say I had it all figured out, but I don't. And I just got some new information that makes me even more concerned. I thought I only had two suspects to think about, but now it turns out there could be three."

Simon looked at him curiously. "I thought you were pretty sure it was that boy with the red pickup truck – that Hoskins boy."

"Well, it turns out that the Hoskins boy has a solid alibi for the night the boy was poisoned. He was at a movie with someone, was seen there, and even has the ticket stubs from that night," Thomas said and sighed. "So, the police have him for the poaching charges, the reckless endangerment charges for shooting at the house, and some other things, but they don't think he is the murderer."

"But what about that night someone shot at the boy out there with the deer?" Simon asked.

145

"It turns out that was a .30-06, and the Hoskins boy only has access to a .30-30, anyway. And there's no evidence that says he was there with a borrowed gun, so that doesn't work."

"So, who are the other two suspects?"

"You know, it really is three more. A boy named Brian Benson, who was one of the boys with Hoskins and who had a grudge against Eddie." Thomas ticked off the name on a forefinger.

"Second, Charles Rothstein, the owner of the property across the road where the deer ..."

Simon's eyes opened wider and he interrupted Thomas. "You mean that rich feller with the big house out on Fiddler Road?"

"I don't know where Mr. Rothstein lives, but he is very well off and he owns several businesses in town. He is suspected of having captive trophy deer hunts on his land across the road. It is thought that he may have worried that Eddie saw too much while he was over there in the field, and might report him. He could be the one who shot at Eddie, and one of his businesses is that customization shop on Randolph Street. The boy was poisoned with a chemical which most people wouldn't have access to, but which is used in that shop for plating metal."

"My Lord! That'd sure stir up a stink, for a feller like that to be arrested for somethin' like murder, especially murder by poison, or even the captive huntin' charges!" He sat back in his chair, scratching his head. "But to kill somebody to keep from being charged with captive huntin'? That seems like too much of a reaction, pastor!"

"Well, you have to look at it from his viewpoint, Simon," Thomas said. "First of all, he's a proud man, and the thought of being humiliated in front of his friends and associates could be a terrible thing for him. And he's a businessman. If his reputation became soiled, he could lose a lot of business – maybe enough to hurt him financially." Thomas paused. "And, there's something else."

"Those deer acted almost tame," Thomas continued, "like they hadn't a care in the world. Eddie could simply stand beside them and touch them. I wonder if maybe Rothstein drugged the deer to make them tame, and make them easier to shoot. That would make his reputation suffer even more, if it came out." Thomas spread his hands. "So, you see, it could cause severe problems for him."

Simon grunted, a frown on his face. In a few seconds he said, "Murder's a terrible thing, pastor, but to me it's almost as bad to drug them deer and shoot 'em while they're that way. That's a pretty lowlife thing to do. I reckon Rothstein could be ruined around here if it got out he'd done that. He'd prob'ly lose two-thirds of his local customers, even if he didn't have anything to do with killin' that boy!"

Simon looked up at Thomas. "And who's the third one, pastor?"

"There's a boy who works in Rothstein's Customizations – that's where the poison that killed Eddie is available. Well, this boy had a small grudge against Eddie, but the most telling thing is that another student saw him acting in a suspicious manner. And he was the one who took care of all the props for the play – including the glass the murdered boy drank from."

Simon leaned back in his chair, eyebrows raised. "You got yourself a real tangle there, pastor. What do you think you ought to do now?"

Thomas was silent for a few seconds, then said in a pensive voice, "I wonder if I shouldn't just give all this information over to the police and let them handle it. But I feel such a burden about trying to help solve the problem myself. When I think about that young man, dying on the stage, his throat being burned by the chemical, and all of us around him applauding his fine acting because we thought he was pretending to die…"

Thomas stopped and swallowed. "It must have been terrible to lie there in such pain, and have everyone around you ignore it, because they didn't think it was real."

Simon leaned forward. "You couldn't have stopped it, pastor. You couldn't have saved the boy's life." Simon's face was twisted by painful memories, and his cheeks were damp. "I remember watchin' Emily in those last few days – feelin' helpless, knowin' that the medication wasn't really helpin' her with the pain. It's a horrible feelin'. Believe me, I know how that guilt feels.

"But I also learned to accept that I couldn't save Emily, either. It was hard, but I had to learn it." The old man's face wrinkled and he looked down at his hands. "I had to. And you have to accept that, too, pastor. You didn't know, so you couldn't have saved him. Even if you knew, how could you have saved him? You can't feel guilty about what you can't control."

Thomas looked at Simon, surprised at this depth of sharing. "Thank you, Simon. You're right, of course. I'm glad you reminded me of that." They both stood up, and walked to the door.

"I'm glad you came by here, Simon. Sometimes it helps to put things together, just to tell someone else about them. It makes you remember the details," Thomas said as he walked out the door with Simon. They went to the old truck Simon was driving. "This isn't your usual truck, is it?"

Simon got into it and buckled his seatbelt. "Nope. They still have my newer one at the shop, redoing the inside. I just got it back from the police about a month ago. Remember, they had it for evidence." He started the older vehicle, which coughed at first, then rattled a little as it slowed to an idle.

"This 'uns sort of a rustbucket, but it's one I had in the barn for rough work. Haulin' lumber, that sort of thing. It looks awful, and runs rough, but it'll get me around till I get my good truck back." He patted the steering wheel.

Thomas stepped back and looked at the rattletrap pickup. It had quite a few rust spots and scratches on the body. As his eyes went over the wheels, something clicked in his mind.

"Simon, I'd like to try to get some information from that young man at the customization shop. They plate hubcaps. I don't have any real metal hubcaps – mine are plastic. But these hubcaps," and he pointed at the ones on the old pickup. "They are the real thing! Could I borrow them, if I promise to bring them back?"

Simon shut down the truck engine and got out. "Don't see why not, pastor." He retrieved a large screwdriver from under the bench seat of the truck and within a couple of minutes had popped off all four hubcaps. "There you go. What are you gonna do with 'em, anyway?" he asked as he handed the stack of hubcaps to Thomas, like a set of rusty, dirty platters.

"I'm going to see about getting them gold plated!"

Chapter 13

The integrity of the upright shall guide them: but the perverseness of transgressors shall destroy them.
$$\textit{Proverbs 11:3}$$

The next morning, Thomas cleaned the rust and dirt from Simon's old hubcaps, making them look as presentable as possible. He knew Theo Rosen wouldn't be at the shop until the afternoon, but he had plenty to do.

After his normal morning study and prayer, Thomas called Eric to let him know about the latest information. Eric wasn't available, so Thomas left a voice mail. It wasn't more than fifteen minutes before Eric called back, though.

"Thomas? You left a message for me to call you. What do you need, or maybe, what have you found out?" Eric asked.

Thomas condensed the information he had gotten from Esther, about Theodore Rosen. Eric made small confirming grunts as Thomas went through all the details.

"And, I happened to drop in on Rothstein's Customization shop. I asked them about getting my hubcaps plated. I looked like a fool at the time, because my hubcaps are plastic, but I didn't know it.

"The important thing is, I asked what sort of plating process they use there. They said they use both electroplating and electroless. The electroless plating is what makes use of the cyanide compounds, like sodium cyanide. The weird thing is, Theo Rosen waited on me when I was there, and at the time, I had no idea about his connection with the play."

"Hmmph! This makes things a little more complicated, but it still puts a lot of focus on that customization shop. Seems like things are converging there, doesn't it?" commented Eric.

"I'm not sure yet, Eric," Thomas demurred. "But, it does seem like that place is a focal point, since we know the poison could have come from there. Have you gotten the results back from the lab on the stuff that poisoned Eddie?"

He heard the annoyance in Eric's voice as he answered, "No, not yet! I don't know what takes them so long. I sometimes think the state crime lab feels the small towns couldn't have any important crimes, so they go to the back of the line."

Thomas heard another phone ring in the background, and Eric said, "Can you hold for a minute, Thomas?" and disappeared without waiting for an answer. Within seconds, however, Eric was back.

"Thomas, I'm sorry. I have a meeting that I'd forgotten, and I'll be late if I don't go right now. Let me know if you learn anything else, OK?"

"Will do, Eric. Talk to you later."

After lunch, Thomas had made up his mind that he would go ahead and carry out his plan with the hubcaps. He would go in and ask for an estimate for getting them gold-plated, making sure he dealt with Theo.

While talking with him, he'd bring up the poisoning at the school, and see what Theo's reaction was. If he didn't react at all, which was unlikely, Thomas would be back to square one. But if he acted guilty or in any way suspicious, Thomas would… well, he'd make up his mind on that when it happened.

Dressed in jeans, flannel shirt and jacket, Thomas got out of his van with a paper grocery bag in his hand. Inside the bag was one of the hubcaps – the rest were laying on the floorboard of the van, in case they were needed. Looking in through the front of the shop he could see that Theo was there behind the counter, though he was on the phone at the moment. Thomas took a deep breath, then entered the shop.

Thomas sort of eased to one side of the shop, looking at the different types of mirrors and other trim they had on display, keeping a watch on Theo out of the corner of his eye. When he saw the boy hang up the phone, he ambled over and stood in front of the counter, waiting to be acknowledged. It took about half a minute, but finally Theo looked up and grinned with recognition.

"Good afternoon again! Did you decide what to do about your hubcaps?" he asked.

Thomas sat the paper bag on the counter. "This time I have a different set of hubcaps that I'd like to get an estimate on. They're for a classic pickup, and I'd like to see about getting them cleaned up and then gold-plated."

The boy's eyebrows went up, but he nodded. "Show me what you have, then, and I'll tell you whether or not we can do it, and if we can, I'll write up an estimate."

Thomas removed one of the hubcaps from the bag. He had chosen the least beat-up looking one of the four, and after cleaning it with abrasive cleanser and a steel wool pad, it didn't look all that bad to him.

The boy picked up the hubcap and eyed it like a connoisseur. "Wow. 1966 Ford, right?" He didn't wait for an answer. "It's not in such bad shape. Let me take it into the back for a second," he requested, and when Thomas nodded, he disappeared for about a minute through a swinging door.

He was smiling when he returned. "I checked with the guy who does most of the gold plating, and he said we would have no problem plating this hubcap." The boy looked down at the hubcap as he rotated it in his hands. "Must be a special pickup to want to do this for it! You said you wanted a quote on getting four of them plated, right?"

"It's pretty special, alright," said Thomas. "And yes, a quote for four hubcaps." He watched the boy as he got out a pad and began to write up the quote.

"You look pretty young to be doing this sort of thing," Thomas ventured. "I'd guess you are still in school, not working in a place like this. Looks like you know what you're doing, though."

Theo looked up with a proud smile. "Well, the manager is my uncle, so I've been around here for a long time. And I do go to school, in the mornings. This is part of my classes, too. It's called DCT." He bent his head over the paperwork again.

Thomas nodded. "Yeah, I've heard of DCT before. You go to school in the mornings, and work in the afternoons, right?" The boy nodded as he wrote. "What school do you attend?" Thomas asked.

"I go to the school at Temple Beth Shalom," Theo said, turning over the hubcap and copying something from the back of it.

"Yeah? That's interesting! I was there the other night for a play. But the play didn't get to finish. One of the young actors died – poisoned, they say." Thomas said all this in an offhand manner, but he closely watched Theo for any reactions.

The reaction was there, alright. Theo stopped writing as soon as Thomas mentioned being at the school for the play, and his hand started to shake when Thomas said something about the poisoning. The top of the pen wiggled so much, it was doubtful the words being written would be legible later.

"Did you know the boy who was killed?" Thomas asked in a quiet voice.

"Um, yeah. I kinda knew him, not much though." Theo was sweating now, and he kept stopping and looking up at Thomas, as though he expected him to strike him or something. He wiped his forehead with his sleeve.

"I, uh, I need your name and address for this quote, sir," Theo said in a shaky and uncertain voice.

"Sure, no problem. Thomas Wilson, 1401 Holly Creek Road," Thomas told him.

"Okay, sir, here is the quote. This is the cost of the labor, here is the cost of materials, and here's the tax." Theo's hand shook all while he pointed out the various charges on the quote. "Our quotes are always good for thirty days, but after that you'd have to get a new one."

Thomas took the quote in his hand and looked at it. "Hmmm. Materials. So that means the gold, right?" He looked at Theo, who nodded without saying anything.

"And maybe the chemicals, too, like sodium cyanide?" Thomas asked, locking eyes with the boy.

Most of the color drained from Theo's face. "Sodi… sodium cyanide?"

"Yes, sodium cyanide. I understand it's used in the electroless gold plating process here, right?" Thomas took a wild shot.

It apparently hit dead center. "Uh, well, yeah… I guess so… yeah, yeah, they use it back there," Theo stammered.

"That's wicked stuff," Thomas commented. "You can't play around with it. Kills very quickly." Thomas smiled at the agitated boy. "Hope you manage to stay away from it yourself. It could be dangerous for you." He picked up his paper bag, dropping the hubcap back into it, and placed the quote in his pocket. "I'll let you know about the hubcaps."

On the drive home, Thomas ran through all his options. About halfway to the parsonage, he turned around in a service station parking lot and went instead to the police station. There, he caught Eric just as he was about to leave the building. They walked to Eric's car together, with Thomas giving him a fast rundown on what he did at the customization shop.

When he was through, Eric just stood and looked at him for a few seconds, with his hands on his hips. He found his voice and said, "I appreciate the help, but you are NOT the police. You could get into trouble with what you are doing, and even mess up the investigation." Eric's face was troubled.

This reaction surprised Thomas. "Eric, look – I'm sorry. I didn't mean to cause any problems and…" Eric held up a hand to interrupt him.

"Thomas, I don't know if you have caused any problem yet or not. But you have certainly stirred up a hornet's nest. And think of the situation you have put yourself in: you went in there, you communicated that you know the boy was poisoned, you know that they use the kind of poison in that shop, and you let that kid know that you know he had contact with the one who was killed.

"And you gave him your name and address, Thomas! What were you thinking?" Eric's face looked angry, now. "If you aren't worried about yourself, at least think about the safety of Amy and little Deanna!"

Thomas's face went pale. "Do you think someone might try to hurt my family or me?"

Eric was incredulous. "Thomas, listen to yourself. That Hoskins kid shot at your house with 12-gauge buckshot just because you put up a security light that kept him from getting a good shot at those deer. What kind of risk do *you* think you are taking, by letting a suspect know that you think he could be involved in a murder, and then giving him your home address?"

Thomas's mind was a jumble of anger at himself, fear for Amy and Deanna, and prayers to God for their safety. "Eric, I'm sorry. I just wasn't thinking. I'm heading home right now. I'll get Amy and Deanna, and we'll go to a church member's house tonight, until we figure out what to do."

"You do that, Thomas. I've already been working on a warrant for that shop, to get a sample of the sodium cyanide which we now know, thanks to you, that they do have there. I'll pick it up now, and we'll be there at that shop within the hour.

"And, with the other information I have from you and Esther, I believe I can talk the DA into an arrest of Theo Rosen on suspicion of murder, or at least complicity in the murder. We'll see." Eric got into his own car and drove off toward the court house, while Thomas almost ran back to his vehicle.

All the way home he prayed. *Lord, have I walked into a place where you didn't lead me? God, take care of my family. Don't let them be punished for my stupidity, Lord!*

Thomas pulled into the parsonage driveway much too quickly, tires squealing on the pavement. The door opened quickly, and Amy stared out at Thomas as he jumped from their minivan and almost ran up the steps.

"Thomas, what's wrong? Why are you driving like that?" Her face was startled at first, but as she saw the look on Thomas's face, it changed to fear and anxiety.

"Honey, don't ask a lot of questions right now. Just grab a change of clothes, toothbrush, that sort of thing, and whatever Deanna might need for an overnight stay. We're leaving now, and I'll explain it after we're on the road. Please, don't ask!" he pleaded as she started asking questions. She looked at him for a few seconds, then nodded.

"Okay. I'll get Deanna's stuff together, if you will get ours. Just grab some jeans, sweater and the other necessities for me," she said and rushed for the back of the house. In less than ten minutes she was in the kitchen with Deanna in her carrier, a diaper bag and a small overnight bag.

Thomas soon followed with another bag, and the cell phone. They rushed out the door and into the minivan, and after they pulled out of the driveway, Thomas picked up the cell phone and put it in Amy's lap. "Call Stan Bowman, honey. He has that big place, and all his kids have moved out on their own."

Without questioning, Amy dialed the number and handed the phone to Thomas.

"Stan? This is Pastor Wilson. I'm alright, but I'm in a little bit of a jam right now. Here's the situation…" and Thomas ran through the highlights of what had happened in the last couple of days.

"So, the detective said the people who did this, whoever they are, might decide that I was dangerous to them, and try to harm me or my family. They have my address."

"My Lord, pastor! What can I do to help?" Stan asked.

"Well, do you still have an empty bedroom that isn't being used? We need a place to stay the night, until we are sure they have picked up the suspects and have them in custody. We may not even have to stay all night, if they get them all in time, but it's just a precaution," Thomas explained.

"I have two bedrooms with beds in them that are not being used. You and your family are welcome to stay the night, or longer if need be!" Stan assured him.

"I hope that won't be necessary. But we appreciate your hospitality and generosity, believe me! We'll be there in a few minutes. I just have to stop at the grocery store for some formula and disposable diapers."

Stan chuckled. "Even in the midst of life and death struggles, babies still need caring for, don't they, pastor? Reckon you and Amy are learning that now!"

Thomas laughed. "Yes, they do. And thank you again!" He shut off the cell phone and handed it back to Amy.

Amy sat through this entire exchange with Stan without saying a word, but her eyebrows shot up and her eyes opened wider. Now, she spoke. "Thomas! Why didn't you tell me this?"

"We didn't have time, honey, or rather, I didn't know if we had time. Eric was concerned for your and Deanna's safety, and he agreed with me that getting all of ourselves out of the house for tonight would be a good idea."

"But just for tonight, right?" she asked, looking at him sharply.

"Honey, as far as I know, yes. Tomorrow morning I'll talk with Eric on the phone, or maybe tonight, and we'll know for sure." Thomas signaled a turn, and went into the parking lot of Wiggleston's grocery. "Do we need formula and diapers, honey? I wasn't sure about that, but I didn't want to impose on Stan's hospitality without bringing along some food, you know?"

She nodded, understanding. "Good idea, Thomas. I think I have enough formula with us, but it never hurts to get a few more diapers. Just get one of the small packs, though. I'll stay here with Deanna."

Thomas hurried into the store, picking up some fried chicken from the deli, some milk, soda and diapers. He carried it all back to the minivan in two bags, but stopped in shock when he arrived there. The doors were locked, and there was no one in the vehicle. Thomas whirled around, looking for any sign of where Amy and Deanna might be. He saw nothing, not a clue.

The first lightning bolt of horror hit his heart. *My God, they've taken Amy and Deanna!* He dropped both bags to the pavement, shaking. Then he heard a voice behind him, calling his name.

"Thomas? Thomas, what's the matter?"

He spun around, stumbling. It was Amy, with Deanna in her arms, and the diaper bag hanging from her shoulder. "Is something wrong, honey?" she asked as she walked to him. It was plain that she had no idea how much terror he had been in for a few seconds.

Dumbly, he shook his head and picked up the bags. Amy unlocked the doors with the key remote in her hand, and they all got in, Amy buckling Deanna into her car carrier.

After she seated herself in the van herself, she looked at Thomas. His face was still a shade or two lighter than usual, and she frowned. "Thomas, something is wrong! What is it?"

He extended a hand for the keys, and fumbled with getting them into the ignition. He started the car, then sat with the engine running. Taking a deep breath, he said, "I got back here and you and Deanna were gone. With all that has been going on… I thought that maybe…" and he stopped, looking at her.

Sorrow and surprise mixed on her face. "Oh, honey, I'm so sorry! Deanna had a really messy diaper, and I didn't want to keep it in the car. So, I went up there and tossed it into the grocery store's restroom trash. I didn't even think about frightening you. Forgive me?" She reached out a hand to take his, and he squeezed her fingers.

"It isn't just the fear, Amy. I had a feeling just then that I don't think I've ever experienced before." He took a deep breath. "When I thought someone had taken you and Deanna, for a moment I was ready to kill someone. I could have struck anyone down, if I thought that person took you two from me, or harmed you." His voice was shaky. "I've never felt that sort of rage before. I didn't know I could."

Amy unbuckled her safety belt and leaned across the vehicle to put her arm around Thomas's shoulders. "Honey, it's only natural, isn't it? To want to protect the ones you love?" She leaned over and kissed his cheek. "You're a minister, but you're a human being, too, Thomas. You can't banish all emotions. You shouldn't want to. God created us in his image, and he said he is a jealous God. He protects those he loves, too. Remember the Children of Israel and the pursuing Egyptians? God didn't hold back his hand from destroying those who were trying to harm and enslave his people."

Thomas turned to look at Amy. "Darling, every time you say something that encourages and lifts me like that, every time you help to keep me on track, I thank God that he brought us together." Thomas squeezed her hand once more, then put their van in gear and drove from the parking lot.

But as he drove, he still wondered, *If I were put in that situation, where it was kill or let my wife and child be taken, what would I do? Lord, what would you WANT me to do?*

Chapter 14

Be merciful unto me, O God, be merciful unto me: for my soul trusteth in thee: yea, in the shadow of thy wings will I make my refuge, until these calamities be overpast.
Psalms 57:1

Thomas and his family arrived at Stan's house without any further incident, though Thomas's mind and heart were still troubled by the overpowering anger he had momentarily felt. Amy had reassured him by reminding him of his human frailty, and he knew that God's strength was made perfect in weakness, but still… what *would* he have done, if the situation had presented itself?

Stan had prepared one of his extra bedrooms, moving an old table out of the way to make room for their things. Amy hugged him in thanks, and he gruffly replied that it was the least he could do.

They all sat down to the fried chicken and potato salad Thomas had purchased, along with some green beans and rolls from Stan's larder. About halfway through the meal, Thomas's cell phone rang. He excused himself and went into the living room to answer it.

"Reverend Wilson here," he said.

"Thomas, this is Eric. Everything OK?" he asked.

"Fine, fine, Eric. Why?"

"Well, I couldn't locate you at your house, and although I hoped you had taken my advice, I still wanted to see if everything was still alright."

"Thanks, Eric. Did you manage to pick up the Rosen boy?"

"We did. And he is sweating bullets in an interview room, right now. His parents are here, as well as a lawyer, but the DA is firm that we have enough to hold him overnight if necessary. The parents are by turns furious and frightened, and the lawyer is, of course, being a lawyer."

"Has he admitted anything?"

"No, but we haven't really begun to pressure him yet, either. He's being allowed time to discuss things privately with his parents and his lawyer, and boy, have they been discussing!" There was no humor in the chuckle Thomas heard on the phone.

"Have you gotten the tests back from the lab yet?" Thomas asked.

"Yep, and that's one of the big guns we will bring out. We picked up samples of the chemicals used in the plating shop there, all the chemicals, and the test on the contents of the Kusack boy's stomach confirms that the sodium cyanide there was of the same type used in the shop. Maybe not the same brand, but the same type." There was satisfaction in Eric's voice.

"You know, we owe a lot to you for pushing into the dark corners that we were ignoring, Thomas," Eric admitted. "And you and Amy were able to connect with Esther when our female detective couldn't. She had some very valuable information that we might not have gotten without your help."

"Look, Eric, I just want this person stopped. If they will poison someone like Eddie, who knows who else may end up dead. You know as well as I do, the first murder is hard, but once you get over that hump, it gets easier for the second and third ones."

"Yeah. Well, I have to go and speak with the Rosen boy and his parents in a minute, but I wanted to check on you."

"Thanks again, Eric. Say, how long do you think we need to hide out?"

"With the amount of sweat the Rosen boy is spilling in there, I'd bet that since we have him in custody, it will be safe for you to go home. BUT," and he emphasized the word, "don't go home yet. I'll let you know tomorrow, okay?" And they hung up.

Returning to the table, Thomas shared what Eric had told him with Stan and Amy. Stan was still flabbergasted that someone had actually poisoned the Kusack boy, and even more so to think that another student might have done it.

"You know, I went in that shop once about a year ago. I was looking for a new mirror for my 1972 Mustang – someone had stolen mine while it was parked in town!" He shook his head at the perfidy of someone to steal a part from a classic Mustang. "They had a lot of parts, but they had to order my mirror for me. I think I remember the boy you are talking about. He didn't wait on me, but I remember him because he seemed to be knowledgeable for someone so young, talking to the customer he was dealing with."

Thomas nodded. "Oh, there's no doubt he knows his cars. He recognized the hubcaps I took in there immediately, both the manufacturer and the year!"

"Are the police and district attorney sure that the Rosen boy is the murderer?" Amy asked, slowly rocking an increasingly sleepy Deanna.

"I don't know, Amy. They must be fairly sure of his guilt, or at least his involvement, or they wouldn't have gone to the trouble of apprehending him and bringing him in for questioning," Thomas said. "Although, I still wonder about both Rothstein and Brian Benson."

"Why is that, pastor? I mean, you're the one who put them onto the Rosen kid in the first place, right?" asked a surprised Stan Bowman.

"It's hard to explain. You should have seen the boy when I asked him about things. When I brought up the play and the death of Eddie Kusack, he started shaking, he was so upset. And when I asked him about the sodium cyanide, I thought he might faint!"

"But doesn't that make him seem that much guiltier, Thomas?" Amy asked.

"Guilty, yes – but not necessarily a murderer. I seriously wonder if he would have the nerve to pull off something like that. It takes a lot to hold someone's death in your hands, and then deliver it to them, I would think. Even when it's as silent and impersonal as poison left in a glass," Thomas said, looking at his own glass of tea as he spoke.

"Then who do you think did it, pastor, if not the boy?"

"Well, let's look at things. First of all, I wonder about Charles Rothstein. Those deer in his field were acting abnormally tame, there's no doubt about it. And there's also no doubt that he had hunters there who managed to bag four trophy deer with four shots, within the space of thirty minutes. What kind of odds are those?"

"Pretty slim ones, pastor," said a grim-faced Stan Bowman.

"Exactly. Now, if he thought Eddie would expose his crime, and make him either a laughingstock or ruin his reputation, his business could suffer greatly. He is a man with a lot of money, but men like that need to have a lot of money coming in, too. In a town like this, with the kind of status that the true deer hunters have, to be found out as a person who shoots drugged or tame deer in a pen would be death for any local business relations!"

Amy wondered aloud, "Do you really think it would hurt him that much?"

Stan answered that question. "Amy, I remember about 15 years ago, a fellow in Plainville, about twenty miles from here, got caught setting bait for deer and shooting over the bait. He had killed several deer that way when he was caught." Stan shook his head.

"It ruined him completely. He started out with his own business, and he ended up having to sell it and move out of state. The word gets around in these communities where hunting is a big thing. Nobody's perfect, but no real hunter believes in being unfair and unsportsmanlike in such a blatant way. They may laugh about miscounting the tines on some antlers, or adding an inch or two to the length of a trout, but when it comes to doing something that lowdown, people remember."

"Yes, I've noticed that a lot of people around here have some very strong opinions about hunting and fishing," Thomas said, and Stan laughed. "I've wondered about Brian Benson, too.

He is the kind of hothead, I think, who would do something stupid and vicious like poisoning Eddie. He was very hostile to me the night of the play, and all I was trying to do was get him to stop bothering Larry and Esther." The other two nodded as they listened.

Thomas took a sip of his tea. "And, I wonder, is that his normal way of acting? That makes him a dangerous person to be around – a bomb waiting to go off. But maybe it was made worse by being under some sort of pressure. Maybe it was the pressure of knowing he had just poisoned someone to death. The murderer, whoever he or she was, had to be feeling some anxiety about being caught, or perhaps being seen while putting the poison in the glass."

"But doesn't that make Theo Rosen the perfect suspect, then? He would have had complete access to all the props, the glasses, the fake liquor – all of it! And no one would question his touching or changing a glass on the set. It would be natural. And he didn't have to worry about fingerprints, because his fingerprints would have been all over the glasses and other props, anyway!" Amy said, then got up to take Deanna and put her in the carrier to sleep for the night.

Thomas and Stan sat silently until Amy returned and sat down with them. She refilled her own tea glass, then Stan spoke. "But you know, that makes him TOO perfect as a suspect, doesn't it? I mean, only an idiot would think they wouldn't be suspected, especially since he was known to be hostile to the boy who was killed."

Everyone was silent, then Thomas said softly, "Or a patsy, maybe."

"A patsy," Amy echoed, mystified. "In what way?"

Thomas sat his tea glass down on the table and stood up, too antsy to sit still. He began to walk a little bit, back and forth, as he thought out loud.

"Suppose you had some really strong reason for wanting to get rid of Eddie Kusack, or thought you did. Now, you don't want to take the risk yourself. Or maybe you don't have a way to get close to the boy.

"But you DO know someone who is close to Eddie almost every day, and who would be able to very easily slip something lethal into Eddie's prop drink."

"The Rosen kid," Stan said, nodding.

"Right! So, you go to the Rosen boy. Maybe you play up his natural animosity for Eddie, or maybe you convince him that Eddie is a danger to both him and yourself. Either way, you manage to talk him into being the delivery boy for your poisonous package."

"But surely he wouldn't want to kill someone, even with his anger toward Eddie!" protested Amy. "That's so hard to believe, Thomas!"

"Detective Lamonde accused me once of being too much of an innocent, Amy, and maybe I was at one time. Think back to when you were a teenager – all the emotions you were experiencing. Teens feel emotions much more strongly than we adults do, because they are all full of the raging hormones, they are being bombarded on all sides by conflicting messages about sex, drugs, alcohol – and violence.

"How many movies and games that are common teenage fare glorify death, or glorify revenge?" Thomas asked quietly. "How many cheapen life by making it seem easy to take a life and get away with it?" Thomas shook his head sadly. "I think it's a dangerous time of life, teenhood. You want to be an adult, you want to be independent, you want to make your own decisions, and yet you are so open to suggestion because of the constant struggle within. That's why I am so committed to our youth ministry!"

Stan said slowly, "So, you think that this boy could have been talked into poisoning the Kusack kid by someone with an emotional hold on him?"

"Or someone with authority of some kind, maybe someone that Eddie looked up to. Or, maybe he was duped even further. Maybe he thought the stuff he was putting into Eddie's drink was just something to make him high. Maybe LSD or something like that. You know, he tried out for the part that Eddie got. He was upset about that." Thomas paused and looked at them both before he continued.

"If you were the one who wanted the part, and the guy who got it blew the role somehow, wouldn't you feel vindicated? You would be able to say, 'Hey, if I'd been playing the part, I wouldn't have been spaced out! I wouldn't have been high on drugs!'"

Thomas turned on his heel and looked at them both. "I can much more easily believe that sort of thing about Theo Rosen, than I can believe that he consciously and with purpose killed Eddie."

The discussion continued for about another hour without any certainty in the outcome. But Thomas had enough doubt in his mind now about Theo Rosen being guilty of murder, that he intended to speak with Detective Lamonde the next day.

Unfortunately, the next day was Saturday, and Eric would not be at the office without a very good reason. Thomas hated to bother Eric at home, but after fidgeting about it for over an hour, he decided it was important enough to call him. But he decided, as he looked at his watch, that he would wait until at least 10:00 AM.

At the moment the clock showed 10:00, Thomas picked up the phone and dialed Eric's cell number. Eric answered, sounding a little sleepy.

"Eric? This is Thomas. I hope I didn't disturb you in any way."

"No, no," Eric said, yawning again. "I was just up late last night, and haven't stopped yawning since I got up. What's the good word?"

"Well, the good word here is that nobody has tried to bother us in any way, and that Amy, Deanna and I slept very well last night here at the Bowman house."

"That's great, Thomas. The lawyer got them to release Theo Rosen this morning on $50,000 bond. I just got a call about it about thirty minutes ago," Eric said.

"And I want to talk to you about that, Eric," said Thomas. "I wonder if Theo is guilty, after all."

"What?? Did I hear you right?" Eric sounded thunderstruck. "You are the one who led us to him, Thomas! You are the one who showed how much sense it made for him to be the killer! And now you say you don't think he is guilty? Come on, now – make up your mind!"

"Eric, calm down! I'm not saying he is innocent of any wrongdoing, I just don't think he was the one who planned the murder. He just didn't seem to be the type who…" but Eric cut him off, his voice carrying his anger even over the phone.

"Just stop it, Thomas. I had a long night, and I'm tired, and my primary murder suspect got released on bond this morning, and now the person who sold me on the murder suspect is trying to recant! I'm not in the mood for it, Thomas. I really am not." And Eric hung up.

Thomas stared at the phone in his hand until it started making the annoying, loud staccato sound that meant the phone should be hung up. Thomas did so, and walked outside to think. He stared up at the remaining brown leaves that dangled from mostly-bare limbs, and the drifts of leaves piled in the ditch, all ready for burning.

Finally, he turned and went back into the house. "Amy, I'm going over to the parsonage and check on things there. I want to make sure there are no problems, get the mail, that sort of thing. I'll be back shortly, OK?" he told his wife, and gave her a kiss on the cheek.

"Okay, honey, but be careful."

As Thomas drove over the narrow country road toward their home, he thought about Eric, about Theo, and about the murder of Eddie Kusack. Theories and possibilities chased each other around inside his head, until it was very hard to separate what he thought might be true from what he knew to be true.

Thomas pulled into the driveway of the parsonage, and got out of the minivan. His mind was still focused very much on the murder and who might be guilty. Almost automatically he walked up the steps and unlocked the kitchen door, entering and dropping his keys into his pocket. He flipped on the light and stopped dead still when he saw that the kitchen and dining room were totally wrecked!

Thomas continued to stand where he was, in shock over the destruction. Dishes were broken, flour was all over the floor and countertops, and drawers were pulled out of the cabinets, their contents emptied onto the floor. A gallon of milk appeared to have been deliberately emptied in the middle of the dining room table, the empty jug sitting upended in the flower arrangement Amy had there.

Thomas whirled and looked at the door he had just entered. No, it was intact. There didn't appear to be any sign of breaking and entering there. But someone had certainly been there! Thomas slowly walked further into the house, all his senses attuned. A gust of wind blew a swirl of flour around his feet.

As he turned the corner from the kitchen into the den, he felt the chilly breeze more strongly. Where there had been a glass-paned patio door, there was now a dry-farm, rimmed with broken glass. Sitting in the middle of the carpet and surrounded by broken safety glass, was a cinderblock. Someone had decided that the easiest way to get in was to break out the patio glass and simply step inside.

Thomas halted, suddenly tense. What if the person was still here? Thomas started to back up slowly, looking from side to side. Just as he backed into the kitchen, a paper grocery bag was jerked over his head, and someone grabbed the back of his collar. Thomas struggled, but something struck the back of his head, hard, and he fell through stars and fog, into darkness.

Chapter 15

Above all, taking the shield of faith, wherewith ye shall be able to quench all the fiery darts of the wicked. And take the helmet of salvation, and the sword of the Spirit, which is the word of God.

Ephesians 6:16, 17

Thomas slowly came to his senses. He could feel that he was lying facedown on some hard surface – the kitchen floor? There was still a paper bag over his head. He heard a voice raised as though in argument, so he didn't move but lay perfectly still.

"Look, I was here in the house. What did you expect me to do, let him catch me? Besides, I owed him one!" There were a few seconds of silence, then the voice again. "Well, I can't help that! He's out cold, anyway." The voice seemed familiar to Thomas, but he couldn't place it. It was a young voice, male.

"Look, I'm leaving while I can. The only reason he didn't know I was here is that I hid my car behind the church. I'm not going to get caught here." Pause, then, "Don't worry, he's alive. I didn't kill him, even though I'd like to!" Thomas heard footsteps, crunching sounds as the person apparently walked around the kitchen, walking on dumped-out cereal and kicking silverware.

"Yeah, Rosen got let out this morning. It's his fingerprints on the glass, not mine. It was him that put the stuff in the glass, not me." The person laughed a very ugly laugh. "He thought Kusack was gonna get sick and puke his guts out on the stage.

You shoulda seen his face when he came to see me the next day! He was white as a sheet."

There was another pause. "Look, we'll talk about this stuff later. I gotta get out of here while I can, without being seen. Besides," and he chuckled, "I want to leave a little gift for this preacher." The footsteps came closer to Thomas, and he felt a light touch against the inside of his leg. There was a strange sound that Thomas at first didn't recognize. But as he felt a warm wetness on his back and heard the sound of water, he realized what it was. Whoever this was, had unzipped his pants and was urinating on Thomas's back!

Thomas felt the stream of urine move up and down his spine, and anger boiled up in him. Quickly, he whirled onto his side, bringing his legs together and over in a scissors movement. The college wrestling moves from ten years ago hadn't entirely left him.

His legs caught those of his attacker, and better yet, caught him unaware. With a cry of anger, the person standing over him and between his legs crashed to the ground, and Thomas snatched the bag from his head. As he heard cursing, he looked and saw a dark brown head of hair and two blazing blue eyes in a face twisted with hate. It was Brian Benson, trying to get to his feet, and Thomas lashed out with one of his heels, striking Benson on the knee.

Benson cried out again, this time more in pain than in anger. Thomas rolled onto his feet and launched himself at the young man. They collided, rolling across the floor.

"Brian," Thomas gasped out as they grappled, "Brian, I know what you did! I heard you on the phone."

The young man cursed, and tried to reach Thomas's face with crooked fingers. "You kept me from getting to my girl that night, you…" He struggled again, and managed to get one leg free, and kicked Thomas in the chest, rolling him back. Benson jumped up and ran to a corner of the kitchen, snatching up a butcher knife that had been dumped there. He whirled, a wild look in his eyes, and came for Thomas in a crouch.

"You know, huh? Then I got nothing to lose, do I?" The muscular young man advanced as Thomas scrambled to his feet. He looked around for something to defend himself with, anything, while trying to keep watch on Benson. With a cry, the crazed young man leaped at Thomas, raising the sharp kitchen knife as he did.

Thomas grabbed the only thing close to him, the thing he had relied upon so many times for protection He grabbed his large, black study Bible and held it across his chest. The wild thrust of the butcher knife drove it deep through the leather cover and into the pages of the Bible, but not through it.

Cursing like a madman, Benson pulled at the knife to free it, and Thomas went with his motion, pushing forward with all his might. The combined forces of pull and push in the same direction catapulted Benson backward, and he tripped, with Thomas landing atop him. Thomas kept his grip on the Bible, twisting, turning and pushing it in order to keep the knife from being pulled from it and used against him. Benson screamed over and over, "I'll kill you, I'll kill you!" as he fought with Thomas.

Through the sound of the struggle and Benson's screams of rage, Thomas heard some welcome sounds: running footsteps entering the kitchen and the voices of men, calling out, "Police! Drop the weapon! Drop it!" But it wasn't until one the policeman grabbed Benson's arms and forced them to the ground that they were able to disarm him. Thomas rolled back from his struggle with the crazed young man, and looked at the door to see Eric Lamonde standing there, shaking his head but with a sad, contrite expression on his face.

The police hustled a cursing, struggling but now handcuffed Brian Benson out to the squad car, and put him none too gently into the back seat. Thomas sat panting in the flour-strewn kitchen floor, his back against the refrigerator. Eric took a chair from the dining area and brought it over, turning it around and sitting astride it backwards.

"Thomas, I'm sorry. I was in a bad mood when you called, so I ignored what you were trying to tell me. And this," he gestured around, "is the result."

Thomas shook his head. "No, Eric, I think this had already been done by the time you and I spoke this morning."

"But you wouldn't have come over here like you did," protested Eric, "if I hadn't blown up at you that way!"

Thomas considered for a moment, and then nodded his head. "You're probably right. I was upset. I thought I was being foolish, and indecisive. I wanted an excuse to get away from Stan Bowman's house and think, and driving over here was the easiest excuse I could think of." He looked up at Eric, who had a bemused expression on his face. "But how did you happen to turn up here?"

"I called back, about fifteen minutes after you had left there. Amy told me you were coming over here. I was worried about you. I was afraid that you might be right, that you might be walking into something you couldn't handle." He chuckled. "But you seemed to be doing pretty good, I have to admit."

Eric knelt down and picked up the Bible, with the butcher knife still pushed deep into it. Careful not to touch the knife to disturb any fingerprints, he examined them both. "He came at you with a knife, and this is the best defense you could come up with?" Eric asked with widened eyes and a quirky grin.

Thomas laughed, a small laugh but a genuine one. "Eric, I can't think of a better defense in this instance."

* * *

Later, at the police station, Thomas was sitting in Eric's office drinking a cup of coffee. Amy was on her way with Deanna, being brought to the police station by Stan Bowman. Thomas had called her and answered her frantic and tearful questions, reassuring her that God had protected him and that he was uninjured.

Eric walked into the office, scrubbing his hand back and forth across his close-cropped salt-and-pepper hair. He had a frustrated look on his face.

"For a young kid, that Benson is stubborn and hard to break. He refuses to talk about the person you heard him talking to on the phone." Eric sat down and swung around in his chair, putting his feet up on the desk before continuing. "And he refuses to admit anything about Kusack's poisoning. He insists he had broken into your house and when you caught him, he panicked and tried to stab you. He says you attacked him, too, and his nose is broken to back up that part of the story." Eric grinned. "At least you got in a good shot or two."

Thomas frowned and said, "Eric, somebody else knows what Benson did. They were discussing it on the phone, and the other person seemed to be upset with Benson. They were discussing the poisoning, and Benson acted like the other person was upset at him for breaking into the parsonage."

Eric took his feet down from the desk with a thump, just as Amy came rushing in, followed by Stan carrying Deanna in her baby carrier.

"Honey!" She grabbed Thomas and pressed her face against his shoulder. "Why did you take the risk? I was so worried!"

Stan stood in the doorway with Deanna, concern on his face, but relief as well.

"Amy, shhh... I'm fine, I'm fine. I told you, the Lord was with me, no matter how foolish I may have been in going there." Thomas held her close and looked over her shoulder at Stan. "And thanks for bringing Amy down, Stan."

Stan chuckled. "I had to bring her, pastor, or she would have hijacked my car. And I couldn't have her driving in that state – she would have been dangerous!" He reached out and shook Thomas's hand. "Glad to see you are still all in one piece."

"I wish I could say the same for the parsonage. Benson broke into it and tore things up pretty badly. I don't know why, either." He turned to Eric. "Has he said why he was tearing the place apart, Eric?"

But before the detective could answer, Amy took Thomas's shoulders in her hands and turned him around to face her. "Thomas! What are you wearing? That looks like jail prisoner clothing!" She fingered the cloth of the shirt. "Are you going to be arrested, too?"

Eric grinned as Thomas looked embarrassed. "Um, no, honey, I'm not going to be arrested. It's just that, well, let's just say that the clothes I was wearing were not in a condition that made me want to wear them."

"Yeah, believe me, Amy, you wouldn't want Thomas wearing those clothes until they have been cleaned a little," Eric put in. "And to answer your question, Thomas, he hasn't really said exactly what he was doing. We asked him if he was looking for something, and he refuses to say." He motioned Amy to a chair. "I was just telling Thomas how stubborn a customer Mr. Benson is being."

Amy released Thomas and sat down in the chair, and Stan sat the baby carrier down on the floor beside her. Deanna, with the innocence and peace of a baby's conscience, slept on.

"What will be the charges against Benson, Eric?" asked Thomas.

Eric paused a moment, then answered, "At the least, breaking and entering, destruction of property, vandalism and assault with a deadly weapon with intent to commit murder."

Amy's eyes grew round, and her face pale. "Murder! Are you sure he intended to kill Thomas?"

Eric's face was very serious as he nodded. "Yes, Amy, I believe he wanted to kill Thomas. Maybe not when he got there, but after they started to fight. Thomas…" he looked at Thomas, and the minister took a deep breath.

"When Benson and I were struggling, I told him I knew all about what had happened, that I had heard him talking on the phone. He said he didn't have anything to lose, so he grabbed a butcher knife from the floor and tried to stab me with it." He spread his hands. "I had no idea he would attack me with a knife, honey!"

Amy's face grew, if possible, even whiter and she put her hands over her mouth.

Eric said hastily, "But Amy, Thomas did an excellent job of keeping Benson away. He broke Benson's nose, did you know that?" Amy looked shocked, and stared at her husband with what looked suspiciously like a new respect. "And when Benson came at him with a knife, Thomas had grabbed up a Bible for defense. Benson stabbed his knife into the Bible, where it stuck. That's where we came in and broke things up, taking Benson into custody."

"But, what did you mean, you 'know all about what happened'?" she asked Thomas. "What did you hear him talking about on the phone?"

As Thomas started to answer, Eric cleared his throat. "Excuse me, folks, but I need to go back and see about trying to get some more information from Benson. We gave him a personal comfort break and brought him something to eat." Eric smiled without humor. "No sense in giving the attorney a chance to say we mistreated his client."

"He has a lawyer already?" Thomas asked, surprised.

"Oh, yeah. He arrived right before the personal comfort break, and demanded time alone with his client," Eric said. "The parents are on their way from their home, but it will take a couple of hours more before they get here. They're driving because they couldn't get a flight."

Thomas's eyebrows went up. "The Benson boy lives alone?"

"Seems to. He's 19, you know, and a legal adult. He's not in college. His parents have a lot of money, and as far as we can figure out, they are the ones who pay for his apartment. They live near Nashville."

"Does he work at a job or anything like that? Or do they provide him with spending money, too?" Amy asked.

"He works part-time at Bear Paw Sporting Goods, but that can't make a lot of money for him," Eric answered. "We're going to be interviewing all the employees there, too, to see if they saw anything strange about Benson's actions, and just to find out a little more about him."

Stan Bowman was frowning, and he asked, "But, detective, Pastor Wilson just said that he heard this Benson talking on the phone about poisoning the Kusack boy. Won't he be charged with that murder, too?"

Eric sighed. "Not at this point. You see, we only have Thomas's word against Benson's. We'll be checking the phone records on your phone, to see if he called anyone from it during the time you were there. That could corroborate your statement, Thomas, if we could identify who he called. There is a call listed on his cell phone as coming in at around that time, but the phone is listed as a private, unidentified number, so even though we know a phone call came in, we don't know who it was from."

"But doesn't the fact that a phone call was received make Pastor Wilson's statement more believable?" Stan asked.

"Yes, it does, but without a phone number we can't take it any further than that. 'More believable' is not the same as 'incontrovertible' evidence. If we knew who, we could track down the person who called him and put some pressure on that person, you know?"

Stan nodded with understanding. "It has to be pretty strong for them to believe that he really poisoned someone, I guess. Why would a young, strong boy who could do violence with a knife resort to using poison? It's too different."

Eric looked at Stan with surprise and respect. "Yeah, that's just it. Very sharp observation!"

Stan grinned, and Eric headed out the door. "Look, I'll see all of you later. I'll let you know, Thomas, if anything else comes up."

Stan broke in there. "And they will be staying with me for a few days, detective, until we get the parsonage all fixed up and ready for them to stay there again."

Amy turned and started to protest, then the words died as she realized that was probably the best thing. She looked at Eric. "Can we go there and pick up some things, or do the investigators need us to leave the place alone?"

Eric looked at his watch. "I think it will be OK if you go over there now. They have had enough time to take all the pictures and so forth that they need." He sketched a sort of salute, and they all three left.

"Stan, Amy and I are going to the parsonage to pick up a few more things. We'll see you at your house in a couple of hours, I think." He hoisted a plastic bag. "I need to get a change of clothing or two, and wash these things."

So, Stan drove off toward his own house, leaving Thomas, Amy and Deanna to go to the parsonage. Amy was horrified and angry at the destruction. She walked around picking this or that object up, placing them on the kitchen counter or table. When she saw the concrete block sitting in the middle of her living room floor and the broken patio door, she leaned against the wall and cried.

"What was he trying to DO, Thomas? We don't have anything particularly valuable! Why would he cause all this havoc? What did he want?" She gestured around at their wrecked living room and kitchen.

Thomas stood silently for a few moments. "You know, I think maybe he was just mad. I think he wanted revenge for my getting in his way that night when he was trying to speak with Esther, and for 'interfering' in what he had tried to do. Maybe just for being nosey. I don't know," he said as he used the toe of his shoe to nudge a piece of broken glass. "I didn't have any evidence here, or anything like that, that he could have taken." He shrugged. "It's a mystery to me."

With the sort of quiet attitudes that people get when they are in the room of someone who is very sick, Thomas and Amy gathered together enough clothes for three or four days. Amy packed up a couple of grocery bags with supplies – they didn't want to put an undue strain on Stan's larder – and Thomas got his sermon notes, Bible and a second, newer study Bible that he had received for Christmas two years ago. He had loved the study helps and so forth in it, but had been attached to the old one with all its annotations, color-coding and scribbles.

Ruefully he looked at the new Bible, still in it's box. "I guess I get to break it in now," he said as he turned to Amy. "The police kept the other one as part of the evidence."

Amy shivered. "Thomas, I'm just so thankful for God giving you protection and for letting that Bible be within easy reach! I don't want to think about being without… without you," she said as her voice broke and tears trickled down her cheeks again.

Thomas embraced her. "Then don't think about it, honey. I'm alive, you're alive, and Deanna is alive, and we are together, and God has plans for us. Remember what God said in Jeremiah: "For I know the thoughts that I think toward you, saith the LORD, thoughts of peace, and not of evil, to give you an expected end." God has a work for us, and we're not through with it yet!

They took their bundles and boxes and loaded them into the minivan. Amy had decided to do their laundry at Stan's house instead of at the parsonage – being there depressed her too much. So they drove away, heading for Stan Bowman's house. Sitting just out of sight down the road from their driveway was a vehicle with a very curious person in it, who watched their departure with binoculars and cursed under his breath.

Chapter 16

Let darkness and the shadow of death stain it; let a cloud dwell upon it; let the blackness of the day terrify it.
                                                                              Job 3:5

Just as Stan, Thomas and Amy were sitting down to supper, the phone rang. "It always happens," muttered Stan, and he got up to answer it. "Bowman residence," he said in a stern voice. But the tone of his voice changed right away. "Oh, Detective Lamonde. Pastor Wilson? Sure, just a minute."

Thomas got up and took the phone from Stan, then stepped around the corner into the living room. "Eric? What happened?"

Eric chuckled. "Oh, all hell broke loose. It seems that one of the policemen was opening the door to Rosen's interrogation room just as Benson was walking by to go to the bathroom. The Rosen kid caught a glimpse of Benson, and about wet his pants."

"But why? Was he afraid of Benson?"

"I think he was afraid the other kid was here to rat on him, try to convince us that Rosen dreamed up the whole thing. So after about ten minutes of private conferring with his attorney, he decided to spill his guts." Eric took in a deep breath. "And, boy, he had a lot to spill."

"What was it, Eric? Don't keep me in suspense!" Thomas asked.

"I'm not supposed to be telling you this kind of stuff at all, now Thomas, so don't push me!" But his voice was easygoing as he continued, "Benson convinced Rosen that he could dump something into Kusack's drink, and make him sick. That would let Rosen come on stage and play Kusack's part for the rest of the performances, so he'd be a hero."

"Yes, I knew Rosen wanted the part all along – Esther told me that."

"Yeah, well, Rosen said Benson came to him with a bottle of red stuff, said he should dump it into Kusack's drink and that it would make him throw up in a few minutes and make him sick for a couple of days. He knows it was stupid to believe Benson, but the kid seems to have a lot of persuasive ability."

"Anyway, the next day Rosen confronted Benson with what happened, and Benson just laughed at him – said it was too bad that Kusack overreacted to the stuff. Then Rosen threatened to go to the police, and Benson got ugly with him. Said there was no way Rosen could prove he had any part of it, that Rosen was the one with access to the poison, and that his fingerprints were on the glass, not Bensons." Eric's voice was grim. "And he made several lurid remarks about what happens to young boys in prison, that scared the stuffing outta the Rosen kid. So, he just kept his trap shut."

"My Lord!" Thomas said with compassion. "He's just been suffering with all that guilt!"

"Hey, don't feel too sorry for him, Thomas! He killed that boy!"

"But that wasn't his intent, Eric! You know that! Didn't you ever make any stupid mistakes when you were a teenager? Weren't there times you would have made someone else sick, if you had been able to do it with the snap of your fingers?" Thomas asked.

There wasn't any sound but Eric's breathing over the phone for a few seconds, then a reluctant voice said, "Yeah, well, I guess that's true. But it doesn't bring the Kusack kid back."

"And neither will making Theo Rosen bear all the responsibility for his death. Has Benson been confronted with all this yet?" Thomas asked.

"He and his lawyer are reading Rosen's sworn statement in privacy right now," Eric said. "Benson's parents still aren't here yet – they called on a cell phone to say that a bad accident delayed traffic so they were still an hour or more away." He chuckled without humor. "But they were adamant that we should treat their son fairly and with justice." He snorted. "Why is it that parents can't believe their kids do the things they do?"

Thomas sighed. "I don't know, Eric. But I appreciate you calling me and letting me know what is going on." He heard the clink of dinnerware and the murmur of conversation from the other room. "We were just sitting down to dinner, so…"

"Oh, sure! Sorry 'bout that," Eric replied. "Go and eat, and if there's anything important I'll let you know. But I don't think anything more will happen tonight."

Eric was right – the rest of the evening passed without any emergencies.

Sunday morning dawned, and the sun burned off the fog that drifted down from the hillside across the road. Thomas taught a Sunday School class, and then delivered a sermon on faith in the face of adversity. *This is just as much for me as it is for them, Lord*, he silently prayed as he ended the sermon.

Thomas, Amy and Deanna went with Sam and Vivian Kingston to have lunch at the local steak house. It was a favorite after-church lunch spot, and he saw the pastors of three or four other churches there with some of their members. Sam and Vivian were eager to hear about all the things that had happened, and were suitably shocked and outraged at the attempted murder of their pastor and the destruction wrought on the parsonage.

"Don't you worry, Pastor, Sister Wilson – we'll get that place all fixed up good as new!" Sam promised. "And this time we'll put better locks on the doors, as well as some of that unbreakable stuff in the patio door windows." He smiled and looked down at little Deanna. "We don't want this little one hurting herself on broken glass!"

About an hour after Thomas and Amy returned to Stan Bowman's house, Detective Lamonde knocked on the door, his face more grave than usual. He greeted them all in a very subdued manner, then turned to Thomas.

"Is there a place where you and I can talk?" he asked in a low voice.

"Sure," Thomas replied, concerned about the grim expression on his friend's face. They walked into Stan's den and shut the door. Eric sat down on the couch, and Thomas sat down on the edge of another chair across from him. Thomas just sat and waited for Eric to start, praying inside that he would know what to say to help.

After a few minutes, Eric took a very long breath, shook his head and began. "You know, Thomas, I've been doing this for a long time. Working in law enforcement, you know? I've seen a few people killed – usually in the course of a robbery or something like that. But sometimes, it just gets to me."

"What happened, Eric?" Thomas asked softly.

Eric looked up from his hands. "You know how we had the statement from Rosen about the poisoning, and how Benson tricked him into doing it?"

Thomas nodded.

"Last night, we eventually managed to get the rest of the story out of Benson. He argued, and his lawyer argued, but in the end it came down to a combination of what we knew and the evidence we had, plus a little coercion." He smiled a crooked smile with no humor. "We didn't use the rubber hoses, but we did pressure him."

"In what way? What were you able to hold over him? It was just his word against Rosen's, wasn't it?" Thomas asked.

"True, but Rosen makes a more credible witness. We saw Benson acting like a maniac, remember? He was trying to kill you, and screaming threats. And there's something else, too."

Thomas looked mystified, so Eric continued after a slight pause. "Remember the shot that someone fired at Kusack?"

Thomas jerked at the memory, and nodded. "Yes, I remember very well. That officer and I went up and found an empty shell casing afterward."

"Right. Well, we thought that maybe that shell casing might be familiar to Benson, so one of the other detectives brought it around to the interrogation room, in an evidence bag. I stood there in front of Benson and his lawyer and I confronted them with it."

"I said, 'See this empty round? It was found at the scene of an attempted shooting of Eddie Kusack. We've checked it for fingerprints. Do you want us to check the results against your fingerprints, Brian?' I asked."

"The kid just sat there with his mouth hanging open for a few seconds, Thomas. Then he started to shake, and tears started running down his face." Eric's face looked troubled. "He confessed, right then and there, to shooting at Eddie Kusack, and to tricking Theo Rosen into poisoning Kusack."

"But why does that bother you, Eric? You were doing your job!"

Eric looked down at his hands again. "Yeah, I know. I'm not worried about getting Benson off the streets. But I am bothered that he has a history of emotional illness and violence, and the system broke down enough to let him come here and kill someone." He sighed. "That's not the worst, though."

"What else happened?"

"It seems that Benson's father is a business friend of Rothstein's – Charles Rothstein's. The kid was kicked out of two schools, and Benson's father heard that the synagogue school had a good reputation. So, he got Rothstein to sponsor his kid for enrolment there. Rothstein also gave him a part-time job at one of his businesses."

"The sporting goods store belongs to Rothstein?"

"Yep. And it seems that's where Benson got the rifle to shoot at Kusack, too. He already had it in his head that eliminating Kusack would eliminate a romantic rival, so he 'borrowed' a Remington 700 from the stock room, and hid the empty box for it behind some others."

"We had a report of a missing rifle from the sporting goods store – Rothstein made a police report. The ammo didn't get reported as missing because Benson took one shell from each of ten boxes in a case. It wasn't noticed at the store. But we didn't put two and two together, because we didn't see the connection at first. It was a breakdown in communication within the department, and that bothers me, too. After all, I am the chief of detectives for this burg." Eric sounded disgusted as he said this.

Thomas reached out and put his hand on Eric's shoulder. "Eric, you can't take responsibility for everything that goes wrong in your department, or in the county. You don't have that much power! You couldn't see all these things. You're human, you're not God."

"I know that, Thomas. But there's more to the story. Brian told us that, after you told Rothstein about the shooting in the field, and after he found out about you looking around up in the field, he started to panic. So he went back up there himself and looked around for the empty casing. When he didn't find it, he figured you must have it. That's what he was looking for at your house today."

Thomas sat upright, understanding breaking in like light from behind a cloud. "He was afraid I was going to turn it in. He didn't realize that the policeman – Officer Riesling – had already turned it in."

"Exactly. And when he saw you there, his anger and frustration sort of boiled over, and he attacked you. He has a history of violence, Thomas. He almost killed a kid in the first school he was expelled from. It was only his parents' money and influence that kept him out of juvenile court then. He had to go to therapy, though, for almost a year."

"They knew he was that violent?" Thomas was shocked. "And they just foisted him off on an unsuspecting school?"

Eric nodded. "And Rothstein knew his history, too. That's why he put him to use."

Thomas looked puzzled now. "Put him to use? How?"

"Benson is violent, yes, but he improved with the therapy, or so say his parents. When Rothstein found out about the shooting attempt, he must have done a little deduction of his own. He heard Benson ranting about this Kusack boy and how he 'stole' his girlfriend. Benson says it was Rothstein who suggested using Rosen to poison Kusack. He says Rothstein even supplied him with the sodium cyanide. Benson added fruit punch concentrate to it to make it red and cover any scent it might have."

Eric's face was drawn into a horrified mask of disbelief. "My God! How could Rothstein do something like that? What did he have to cover up? Some stupid captive hunting? What makes that worth the life of a young boy?" His mind was spinning.

Eric got up and went to the window of the den, looking out into the gray November mist. "If you had been living at the parsonage today, you might have seen what has been going on over there this afternoon. Two investigative units went up behind that hill. They found a few things.

"They found a pen about 100 yards long and 50 yards wide, made of hog wire. It was about eight feet high. Just outside the pen they found a small shed and some racks that appear to be made for hanging the deer and gutting them. There were signs of blood and buried offal."

Eric turned toward Thomas. "You were right, Thomas. We also found a nice little patch of cannabis sativa – marijuana – growing about twenty five yards away. It was in a fence, too, but had been harvested in the last few weeks." He returned to the couch and sat down. "You know what we found in the locked shed?" Without waiting for an answer he said, "Cattle feed – mixed with lots and lots of marijuana. Over 25% marijuana, in fact."

Thomas was astounded. "So, Rothstein was growing his own marijuana and feeding it to the deer to make them docile! I guess he was very worried, then. The drug charge and the captive hunting charge together could ruin him financially and personally."

Eric took a long, deep breath. "That must be what he thought this afternoon, too."

Thomas could see that there was more than just the thought of Rothstein plotting the murder of a young man, bothering Eric. "Eric, what happened this afternoon?"

Eric got up again. He just couldn't seem to sit still, or even stand still. He walked over to the window, then to a small shelf of knick-knacks, picking up two or three of them and examining them as though looking for flaws. "Eric, what happened?" repeated Thomas in a soft but insistent voice.

"While the investigative units were up there behind the hill looking at the captive hunting setup and finding the drugs, I went with two officers in a black-and-white to Rothstein's house to arrest him. We pulled up in front of the house, and just as we rang the front doorbell, there was the sound of a gunshot.

"We tried the door, and it was locked, so we broke it down. We went in, calling for Rothstein to give up, that we were the police. We found a locked door on the second floor and pounded on it. He was inside that room."

"We called out to him to come out, unarmed, that we were police officers and we needed to talk to him. He sounded very distraught when he yelled back at us that there was nothing else to talk about. Then we heard another gunshot, and the sound of something heavy falling. We entered after breaking down that door, too."

Eric put his hand across his eyes, then removed it. His eyes were very red. "Thomas, both Rothstein and his wife were there. She was dead - shot through the back of the head. She hadn't seen it coming – she couldn't have. She was just sitting in that chair, dead" Eric repeated.

"The window looked down on the driveway. Rothstein was lying on the floor in front of it. He must have looked down onto the drive and saw us when we drove up. The first gunshot we heard was his wife, because her body was still warm. He wrote a note – we found it on his desk. He couldn't stand the thought of being disgraced, or having his actions discovered by his wife, so he killed her and then himself."

There were tears on Eric's cheeks now. "Thomas, this woman could not have known for one instant what was about to happen to her! There was no sign of a struggle, and she was shot from behind. My God, she had a book in her lap, like she was reading it! How could this man, her husband, be so caught up in his own pride that he could destroy his wife that way?"

"Eric..." Thomas began, but the detective turned toward the window again.

"This whole stupid thing – this chain of three deaths – wouldn't have started if Rothstein did what was right." Anger and grief mixed in Eric's voice. "If he reported Benson's theft of the gun, and the attempted shooting of the Kusack boy, Benson would have been arrested, but no doubt committed to an institution for treatment, given his history.

"Sure, Rothstein's involvement with the drugs and the captive hunting MIGHT have come out, but then they might not have. Benson swears up and down he knows nothing about any captive hunting. He only knew Kusack was going up there and messing up the poachers' attempts to spotlight the deer. How he found out about that, we don't know yet, but he admits he knew about it."

Eric turned around and looked at Thomas, his face etched with anger, pain and frustration. "Stupidity! Rothstein couldn't stand for his wife to find out about his screwups, so he blew her brains out, then took himself out, after conniving to kill an innocent young man by manipulating two other young men! Forget the drugs and the captive deer hunt - I couldn't care less about those! But the rest..." Eric shook his head and sat down on the sofa. "Why, Thomas?"

Thomas was silent for a moment. "Eric, people have been asking that question ever since Cain slew Abel. I'm sure Eve asked it, and Mary, and every other person throughout history who saw an unjust death." Eric looked up at Thomas, who continued. "People, unlike what it is now fashionable to think, are not inherently good. All of us have the seeds of doing wrong within us. We make a conscious decision every day NOT to kill, or steal, or rape, or we decide in the other direction.

"All of these people - Rothstein, Benson and Rosen - made their decisions based on their egos. Rosen wanted to be the hero of the play, Benson wanted to regain the girl he regarded as 'his', and Rothstein killed because he was trying to protect his image and his standing in the town." Thomas reached out and placed his hand on Eric's shoulder.

"You have to look at the people who make decisions in the other direction, Eric, or you will lose hope altogether. Kusack did what he did because he was trying to prevent unethical hunters from shooting tame deer. Esther came forward with information to try to capture Eddie's killer and stop him from killing again."

Eric looked at Thomas, adding, "And you dig and dig to find the truth, even when it's not your responsibility, because you believe it's the right thing to do."

Thomas nodded. "I guess so. And you keep doing your job, even when it's hard and thankless and painful, because you know it's the right thing to do, too, don't you Eric?"

Eric heaved a deep breath. "Yeah, I guess so." He stood up, and Thomas did, too. "Thanks for listening to me, Thomas, and for talking to me, too," he said, reaching out to shake the minister's hand. "It's been a long time since I've had a 'heart-to-heart' with a preacher." He grinned crookedly. "It wasn't as hard as I thought it might be."

"Any time, Eric. Any time," Thomas said.

* * *

In the weeks and months following, Holly Creek Christian Church's new facility continued to grow. The new sanctuary and Christian education facilities were dedicated in late January. Eric and Maria were both there for the dedication.

Theo Rosen had a good lawyer, and a sympathetic jury, and ended up with a manslaughter charge. His age and lack of a prior record, plus the confessions of Brian Benson and Charles Rothstein were held as mitigating his crime, and he received a minimal sentence.

Brian Benson also had a good lawyer. But because of his history of violent behavior as well as his murderous actions against Reverend Wilson and Eddie Kusack, he was committed to a state psychiatric hospital. He is due to be evaluated in five years.

The big, fine house on Fiddler Road still sits empty. The murder-suicide that occurred in it is too well-known, and every potential buyer for the place has come away from it with a cold, chilled feeling, so the estate lawyer has decided to let the matter rest for a while.

Maybe in a couple of years, she reasoned, people would forget and she would be able to get it on the market successfully. Until then, a caretaker goes in once or twice a month to check on things, but he never goes into Charles Rothstein's office. At least, not any more. "Just don't feel right in there," was all he would say about it.